D1015642

BUDAPEST

BUDAPEST
A Novel

Chico Buarque

Translated by Alison Entrekin

GROVE PRESS
New York

First published in Brazil in 2003 as
Budapeste by Companhia das Letras

First published in Great Britain in 2004 by
Bloomsbury Publishing Plc, London

Printed in the United States of America

Library of Congress Cataloging-in-Publication Data

Buarque, Chico, 1944–
    [Budapeste. English]
    Budapest : a novel / Chico Buarque ; translated by Alison Entrekin.
        p. cm.
    ISBN 0-8021-1782-1
    I. Entrekin, Alison. II. Title.
PQ9698.18.O35B8313 2004
869'.342—dc22   2004052299

Grove Press
841 Broadway
New York, NY 10003

04 05 06 07 08   10 9 8 7 6 5 4 3 2 1

It should be against the law

IT SHOULD BE AGAINST the law to mock someone who tries his luck in a foreign language. One morning, when I accidentally left the metro at a blue station exactly like hers, with a name similar to that of the station near her place, I called from a phone booth and said: There I am arriving almost. I instantly suspected I'd made a blunder, because my teacher asked me to repeat the sentence. There I am arriving almost . . . there was probably something wrong with the word almost. But instead of pointing out my mistake, she made me repeat it and repeat it and repeat it, then broke into a cackle that made me slam the phone down. When she saw me at her door she had a new fit of the giggles, and the more she tried to contain them, the more her whole body shook with laughter. She finally said she had understood that I would arrive

1

little by little, first my nose, then an ear, then a knee, and the joke wasn't even that funny. Proof of this was that Kriska grew a little sad and, not knowing how to apologise, ran her fingertips across my quivering lips. I can now say, however, that I speak Hungarian perfectly, or almost. Muttering to myself in the evenings, I am deeply unsettled by the suspicion of the faintest of accents here and there. At the venues I frequent, where I speak publicly on topics of national importance, I employ rare verbs and correct highly educated people; a sudden misplaced accent would be disastrous. I have only Kriska to confirm or deny my niggling suspicions, although she is not very trustworthy; to keep me wrapped around her little finger, where perhaps she wants me, she will always hold something back. Even so, from time to time I ask her in secret: Have I lost my accent? Perverse, she replies: little by little, first your nose, then an ear . . . And she kills herself laughing, then regrets it, rubs the back of my neck, and so on.

I wound up in Budapest due to an unscheduled landing on a flight from Istanbul to Frankfurt with a connection to Rio. The airline put us up at the airport hotel and only informed us the following morning that the technical problem responsible for our landing had, in fact, been an anonymous bomb threat. Glancing casually at the twelve o'clock news, however, I had already become intrigued when I recognised the German plane parked on the runway of the local airport. I turned up the volume, but it was in Hungarian, rumoured to be the only tongue in the world that the devil respects. I switched off the TV; it was seven o'clock at night in Rio, a good time to call home. I got the answering machine, didn't leave a message, nor would it make sense to say: Hi, honey, it's me, I'm in Budapest, there's been a hitch with the plane, bye. I should have been tired, but I wasn't, so I filled the bath, sprinkled some bath salts into the warm water and amused myself piling up bubbles. That's what I was doing when, *zil*, the doorbell rang, I still remembered that doorbell in Turkish was *zil*. Wrapped in a towel, I opened the door and found an old man in the hotel uniform holding a disposable razor. He'd got the wrong door and let out a guttural 'o', like that of a deaf-mute, when he saw me. I returned to my bath, and it struck me as odd that a luxury hotel should employ a deaf-mute as an errand boy. But the *zil* stuck in my head; it's a good word, *zil*, much better than doorbell. I was soon to forget it, as I would forget the haikus memorised in Japan, the Arabic proverbs, and the Ochi Chornye I sang in Russian; I pick up a little treasure in every country, a fleeting souvenir. I have this child's ear that latches on to and lets go of languages easily. If I set my mind to it, I could learn

Greek, Korean, even Basque. But I had never dreamed of learning Hungarian.

It was after one when I went to bed naked, turned the TV back on and found the same woman I had seen at midnight, a heavily made-up blonde, presenting a rerun of the news. I knew it was a rerun because I had already noticed the broad-faced peasant woman staring at the camera with bulging eyes, grasping a cabbage the size of her head. She waggled her head and the cabbage up and down at the same time and talked non-stop at the reporter. She dug her fingers into the cabbage, and cried, and wailed, and her face grew redder and puffier and she buried all ten fingers in the cabbage, and by now my shoulders had tensed, not because of what I saw, but from the strain of trying to catch at least one word. Word? Without the slightest notion of the appearance, the structure, the actual body of the words, I had no way of knowing where each one began or finished. It was impossible to detach one from the next; it would be like trying to cut a river with a knife. To my ears, Hungarian could, in fact, have been a seamless language, not composed of words, which only revealed itself in its entirety. And the plane reappeared on the runway in an image that was distant, dark and static, further emphasising the male voiceover. By now I couldn't have cared less about the plane story; the mystery of the plane was overshadowed by the mystery of the language in which the story was presented. There I was, listening to a series of amalgamated sounds, when I suddenly detected the clandestine word, Lufthansa. Yes, Lufthansa; the newsreader had most certainly let it slip, the German word infiltrating the wall of Hungarian words, the opening that would allow me to unravel the entire vocabulary. The news was followed by a round table whose participants appeared to be having a misunderstanding, then a documentary about the bottom of the ocean, with transparent fish, and at two on the dot my made-up friend was back, looking older by the hour. Weather, parliament, stock market, students in the street, shopping centre, woman with cabbage, my plane, and I was already trying to reproduce a few phonemes after Lufthansa. Then a girl with a red shawl and black bun came on, threatening to speak Spanish, and I jumped channels with a start. I got a channel in English, then another, and another, a German channel, one in Italian, then back to the interview with the flamenco dancer. I muted the sound, concentrated on the subtitles and, seeing Hungarian words in letters for the first time, I felt as though I was looking at their skeletons: *ö az álom elötti talajon táncol.*

When my wake-up call came at six, I was sitting on the edge of the bed. Soon I would be reciting the plane story in unison with the voiceover, a good twenty seconds of Hungarian. Then I pulled the previous day's clothes back on with distaste, as we had only been allowed to bring our hand luggage, and went down to the lobby, which had become a Babel. The more the various languages disagreed with one another, the louder were the protests about terrorism, the airline, the extras the hotel was charging. The voices only hushed when the restaurant opened for the complimentary breakfast, but the damage had been done; I went to fetch my Hungarian words in my head and found only Lufthansa. I tried to concentrate, stared at the floor, paced back and forth, and nothing. I spotted a circle of talkative waiters at one end of the restaurant and thought I could at least sponge a few words off them. But when they noticed me they lapsed into a sudden silence and gestured for me to sit with three Slavic-looking giants at a table littered with crumbs, fruit skins, cheese rinds and four tubs of yoghurt scraped clean. A few reddish-coloured rolls remained untouched in the bread basket, undoubtedly a local speciality, which I tried with caution and to be polite. The bread was light and sweet, with a slightly bitter aftertaste. I ate one, two and ended up eating all four because I was ravenous and the things weren't so bad when washed down with tea. They were pumpkin rolls, the maître d' told me in English, but I wasn't interested in the recipe, I wanted to savour their sound in Hungarian. In Hungarian, I insisted, and began to suspect they were jealous of their language, as the maître d' was unyielding. He uttered a guttural 'o', dumped a pile of rejected rolls from nearby tables on my plate and clapped his hands to hurry me up, making me realise the restaurant had emptied. In the lobby, a flight attendant holding a list and a walkie-talkie was yelling Mr Costa! Mr Costa! and I was the last to join the legion funnelling on to the moving pavement thirty feet from the hotel doors. We rolled to the departure gate through a long, luminous no-man's-land, a country with no language, home to numerals, icons and logos. At the Federal Police counter a moustached employee idly flicked through each passport, which he returned unstamped. My last hope of hearing a Hungarian voice melted away, as his lips did not pronounce a single good morning, thank you very much or have a nice trip, much less a hope to see you again soon. Perhaps in compensation, the taste of the pumpkin bread returned to my tongue as I settled into my business-class seat, and it was sweet again. I fastened my seatbelt, closed my eyes, thought I would never sleep again in my entire life, took a sleeping pill and the plane took off. I leaned towards the window, everything was cloudy, the pill was beginning to take effect. When the clouds parted a little, we appeared to be flying over Budapest, divided by a river. The Danube, I thought, it was the Danube but it wasn't blue, it was yellow, the whole city was yellow, the rooftops, the asphalt, the parks, funny that, a yellow city, I had thought Budapest was grey, but Budapest was yellow.

In the case of the children

A NEW TURN OF EVENTS in the case of the children with punctured eyes. Last night the matron of the orphanage, believed to be in hiding in Paraguay, reported to the Volta Redonda police station on her own initiative. The narration dragged, her voice was lacklustre: Vanda had undoubtedly recorded the text very early in the morning. The chief officer refused to say whether the governess's statement could prove the innocence of the seamstress's lover or further implicate him. No, no, nothing conclusive, the woman appeared to be sedated or in a state of shock, her sentences were incoherent, and Vanda came back on live announcing the women's football after the commercials, her voice smooth, with an appropriate half-smile, equidistant from the two news items. She wore eye shadow, her hair back, the bead necklace. I sat on

9

the bed; the answering machine was blinking on the bedside table: Zé, it's Álvaro, you must have already . . . Vanda honey, it's me, Vanessa, the phosphorescent balls . . . Zé, it's Álvaro, look, mate, the German's . . . Vanda, it's Jerônimo speaking, you can call me at the mezzanine. Vanda honey, it's Vanessa, I thought the balls . . . Zé, Álvaro, it's midday, look, mate, you . . . I had drunk wine, swallowed barbiturates, the plane had been delayed in Frankfurt, there had been a stopover in São Paulo, suitcases had gone missing, time zones, jetlag, I showered, ate some bananas, drove slowly along the beach, close to the bicycle path, girls riding, girls on skates, autumn sun, I parked the car in Ipanema. The kiosk was quiet, I ordered a coconut water, folded my arms on the counter, rested my head on my arms, heard people passing back and forth behind me: did you see his face, the prick even went white . . . she pulled down her knickers and there was that wart . . . only top-notch equipment, the full works . . . then they'd say it was for a nigger . . . so I told him I had my period . . . but it was worth a bit of dough . . . the vice president told me over the phone . . . I reckon maybe that's it . . . I thought of taking my shoes off and going for a paddle, but the sea was far away and I couldn't be bothered trudging through the sand. I had to head for the agency, got in the car, laziness over-whelmed me.

Laziness was unknown to me back in the days when we used to consult in a three by four office in the city centre. I was the one who consulted, actually, because Álvaro spent the days out and about, making contacts, seeing to things. Back in the days when he still advertised the agency in the classifieds, he had the word trustworthiness printed in bold. And some edgy types would turn up, looking at the ground and speaking out of the corners of their mouths; I took on any kind of job in those days. Not for the money, which barely paid the rent on the office; they paid me the going market rates, as one pays by the page an old scribe, a typist or an encyclopedia copyist. They paid cash on delivery for the goods and left quickly, at the most half-opening the envelope to check how many pages were in it. For me, those dissertations and theses were an exercise in style, as were the medical science exams, the lawyers' petitions, the love letters, goodbye letters, desperate letters, blackmail, suicide threats, texts I showed Álvaro before wiping the files. He would glance at the screen saying genius, genius, his thoughts elsewhere; Álvaro's thoughts were never exactly on what he was looking at. Vanda took a dislike to him right when we first starting seeing one another, referring to Álvaro as the vampire, because he fed off my talent, because he locked me in the agency and went to cocktail parties. She said this

11

because she cared for me, not my writing, which she never read; Vanda had no real idea what kind of writer I was. She met me when I was already quite well heeled and did not know how much Álvaro had believed and invested in me, from my degree in language and literature to the agency, set up on his initiative. He had some family money, was well connected, and when he hooked up with some guys in politics, I was able to write speeches for any occasion based on notes or a brief interview. Campaign speeches paid well, but left me dissatisfied, unhappy even. Speakers would often mangle the passages I most prided myself on, not hesitating to skip entire paragraphs if their schedules were busy or the sun hot. And they would suddenly toss in ravings of their own, which the commoners applauded, then abandon the papers on the podium for the wind to carry away. Such that I only found true professional reward in the full publication of my articles in widely read newspapers. My name did not appear, of course; my fate had always been to remain in the shadows, but the fact that my words were attributed to a string of illustrious names was stimulating, a means of advancement within shadows. By now the Cunha & Costa Cultural Agency was established in an office suite overlooking Copacabana Beach, and Álvaro took it into his head to frame and hang what he considered my best work. They were articles written in the name of the President of the Federation of Industries, the Minister of the Federal Supreme Court, the Cardinal Archbishop of Rio de Janeiro; in short, it was a gallery that Álvaro exhibited to whomever set foot in the agency, saying: José Costa is a genius. He visited businesses, state companies, foundations, unions, clubs, steak houses, opened a portfolio of my articles and announced: José Costa is a genius. But Álvaro, what about trustworthiness? He laughed his weedy laugh, funny on a large hairy man, and reassured me that our clients were the first to advertise Cunha & Costa. Even non-clients were known to brag that they had dismissed their technical consultants and paid a little more for our premier services; these were Álvaro's words. Nevertheless, the articles on the walls made me uncomfortable, the portfolio made me uncomfortable; being in evidence was something akin to breaking a vow. I indicated as much in a frank conversation, and Álvaro listened with a steady gaze; his thoughts elsewhere. He continued expanding the gallery and hired an employee to carry the portfolio, which by that time was voluminous. At any rate, when boasting of our text factory about town, he was now careful to omit my name. If anyone asked if he, Álvaro da Cunha, was not indeed the versatile man of letters, he would lower his gaze and mutter: Let's not go into that.

After I was married, I would arrive home late at night in a state and Vanda would be indignant, heating up my soup while cursing Álvaro. I didn't contradict her, as I had no way of explaining that after work I hung around the agency alone of my own accord, reading obsessively. In those hours, seeing my work signed by others gave me a nervous pleasure, a kind of reverse jealousy. Because for me, it was not the individual who took possession of my writing; it was as if I had written in his notebook. Night would fall, and I would reread the turns of phrase I knew off by heart, then repeat the name of the individual aloud, and would shake my legs and laugh my head off on the sofa; I felt as though I was having an affair with somebody else's wife. And if my turns of phrase made me puff up with vanity, greater yet was the vanity of being a discreet creator. It was not pride or conceit, naturally silent feelings, but vanity itself, with a desire to boast and show off, making my discretion all the more laudable. And I was commissioned to write new articles, which were published in newspapers with front-page headlines and praised by readers the following day, and I withstood it all. This produced a buildup of vanity inside me, made me strong and beautiful, and caused me to argue with the telephonist and tell the office boy he was stupid, and it ruined my marriage because I would arrive home yelling at

Vanda and she would stare at me wide-eyed, unfamiliar with the reasons for such vanity. I had a positively foul temper by the time the invitation to the annual anonymous authors' convention, to be held in Melbourne, turned up at the agency. The letter had been posted in Cleveland, without any other indication of the sender, and was addressed to Cohna & Casta Agency, in a black envelope that Álvaro opened and handed me, amused. I tossed the letter into the unimportant things drawer, if nothing else because it contained no more information than the name of a hotel and a date that I unintentionally committed to memory: Vanda's birthday. Months later, arriving home at two in the morning, I found my wife sitting up in bed with a sleepy face, since she woke up early now that she was a TV newsreader. When she asked me if I still wanted my soup, I answered on an impulse that she looked like a parrot on television, because she read the news without knowing what she was saying. She put on her slippers, pulled a crocheted cardigan over her pyjamas, headed slowly for the kitchen, turned on the microwave, and without raising her voice said that I was worse, writing scores of things that no one read. I forwent the soup, left home with the shirt on my back and settled into the agency, where I enjoyed the company of my articles until I fell asleep on the sofa. After several nights of sleeping there, with a bit of leftover anger and a sore back, I thought of going back to Vanda because of her birthday, and that was when I remembered the invitation in the drawer. Álvaro was not averse to my trip to Australia and even made a few comments about globalisation and so on and so forth. I had enough money; at over thirty years of age I had never left the country and thought that a plane trip around the world would, at the very least, allow my head to cool. I stopped off at home to pack my suitcase; Vanda wasn't there and I left a note informing her that I was leaving for the world writers' conference.

Ethics, press law, criminal liability, copyright, the advent of the Internet; the conference, behind closed doors in a dingy Melbourne hotel, had an extensive list of topics. Speakers of many nationalities gave a succession of talks, which I followed in Spanish through the simultaneous translation system. On the second day, however, as night approached, issues of common interest began to give way to embarrassing personal testimonies. The whole thing was beginning to remind me of an alcoholics anonymous meeting, whose participants suffered not from alcoholism, but anonymity. Veteran authors, flaunting their full names on their nametags, competed for the microphone in an orgy of self-congratulation. They reeled off a string of their own works, and unnecessarily revealed the identity of the supposed authors: a great statesman, the renowned ghost-writer of a great statesman, a novelist laureate, a philosopher, a prominent intellectual, provoking commotion and guffawing in the audience. On the third night I was actually about to leave the room, when the microphone ended up in my hand and the other participants folded their arms, eyeing me. I was the newcomer, perhaps a strange element. I had heard compromising confessions and there was no way out: my silence would have been an affront. Apologising for speaking in Portuguese, I gave a summary of my curriculum vitae, mentioned my doctor's thesis, was applauded, and agreed to recite some of my turns of phrase slowly, so the interpreters could translate them at leisure. I then explained the background to a couple of my works, alluded to personalities who owed me favours, and soon I was spouting jumbled fragments of any article that sprang to mind. By now it was a compulsion; I ranted, raved, raved, and would have raved on until daybreak had they not switched off the sound system. When I saw the empty room and the packed lift, I darted up seven flights of stairs in one go; I was light, I was lean, and at the top I felt as though I had become hollow. The nausea I felt as I entered the room was to accompany me for a long time to come; the mould of the hallways impregnated my nostrils and for months afterwards, every time I lounged around on the agency sofa to savour old articles, the smell of the orangey carpet of the Melbourne hotel returned to me. My room was stuffy, the window did not open, and the view was two rows of lampposts on a straight, unending avenue. I felt like calling someone in Brazil, but the line was blocked. I spent the night staring at the ceiling, and when breakfast was delivered I was immensely grateful and insisted that the room-service waiter sit with me. He was Filipino and barely spoke English. He taught me a couple of words in Malay and had very small hands, which I stuffed with coins. Feeling emotional, I went down to the conference room anxious to meet up with my colleagues, and from that morning on the sessions took place almost in silence, with people prostrated in their seats. The few who were willing to take the podium spoke quietly, far from the microphone, recalling the hardships of a profession that so many desert in search of popularity and fortune. Homage was paid to absent colleagues, who had died in oblivion or been committed to asylums for schizophrenics, or who had been denounced, publicly identified, some even persecuted in their countries and found guilty of crimes of opinion; professionals who, on principle, have no opinion. In the closing session there were speeches in defence of the rights to privacy and freedom of expression, but the proposal to write an open letter was dismissed out of hand; after all, no newspaper would publish a petition signed by writers who never sign. And we, who a week before had arrived at the hotel slamming taxi doors and lambasting bellboys, departed slowly together, dragging bags bursting with wads of paper to the chartered bus on the other side of the street. At the airport we exchanged addresses and hugs; there were those who cried; everyone swore to be present at the next conference in Casablanca, then each of us entered a tunnel. I travelled for thirty hours with a blank mind, and when I requested to sleep at home, Vanda asked me nothing, served me soup and straightened my hair. That was when, stripped of self-love, I got Vanda pregnant.

With her belly beginning to bulge and full of whims, Vanda decided to plan our eternally post-poned honeymoon. It was to be in New York, during her month's holiday from the news, but I was un-comfortable about asking Álvaro for more leave. Vanda put her foot down, bolstered my sense of self-worth, made me see that I was not his employee, I was almost his full partner. I sat down with Álvaro, showed him my new laptop, spoke of the inflexibility of women in general and in the end he said I could travel if I wanted and even promised to give me a guide to good addresses in Manhattan. And he took the opportunity to say that shortly, if I didn't mind, he would probably be outsourcing some of my duties. I only really got the gist of what he was on about when I got back from the honeymoon, when I found a young writer installed at a desk facing mine and half a dozen of his articles framed on the walls. For some time, as I was to discover, Álvaro had been training the lad to write not as others did, but as I wrote for others, which struck me as misguided. Because my hand would always be my hand; it was as if my gloves wrote for others, just as an actor disguises himself as a thousand characters in order to be himself a thousand times over. I would not refuse to lend an apprentice my accessories; that is to say, my books, my experience and some technique, but Álvaro aspired to pass on that which was more than my property. To avoid becoming irritated, I decided to ignore the lad's texts and sat with my back to his, because it is impossible to create with a stranger staring us in the face. But one night when I was alone in the agency, my eyes wandering across the walls of the reception area, I came across a newspaper article in a baroque frame, and the title The Lady and the Vernacular seemed familiar. I went over for a look; it was a recent article signed by the President of the Brazilian Academy of Letters, for whom, as it happens, I had never written, and could only have been the lad's. I read the first line, reread it and stopped. I had to admit, I could not have introduced that article with any words but those. I closed my eyes, thought I could guess the following sentence, and there it was, word for word. I covered the text with my hands and went along removing my fingers inch by inch, opening words letter by letter like a poker player squeezing his cards, and they were precisely the words I was expecting. I then tried the most unexpected words, neologisms, archaisms, a fucking hell out of the blue, brilliant metaphors that I came up with on the spot, and whatever else I conceived of was already printed there under my hands. It was harrowing, it was like having an inter-locutor that continuously took words from my mouth, it was agony. It was like having a plagiariser who preceded me, a spy in my skull, a leak of the imagina-tion. I began to look askance at the lad and thought of challenging him face to face, pressing him up against the wall, but soon another lad was hired, and another, and Álvaro succeeded in imposing my style on all of them, almost leading me to believe that my own style, back at the beginning, had also been the result of his manipulation. When I found myself surrounded by seven writers, all wearing striped shirts like mine, with reading glasses just like mine, all with my haircut, my cigarettes and my cough, I moved into a small room behind the reception area that was being used as a storeroom. There I recovered my taste for writing, as the newspaper articles depressed me; I felt as if I was imitating my emulators. I began to create autobiographies, which Álvaro encouraged, stating that it was a kind of merchandise for which there was much repressed demand.

Artists, politicians and crooks came knocking at my door, but I permitted myself the luxury of working only for individuals as obscure as myself. Clients who reminded me of those from the three by four office in the city centre, except that they were rich enough to afford Álvaro's exorbitant fees and finance the printing of the book for distribution among family and friends. Individuals such as the old zebu breeder from the back of beyond, whose memoirs I rewrote with lots of sex, transatlantic steamers, cocaine and opium, affording him some comfort in a hospital bed. The man really was at death's door, and barely had the strength to autograph a copy of his *Passionate Inventory*, which I took to the anonymous authors' convention in Istanbul. I selected the best passages to read in public, but my peers demanded that I read it from cover to cover; although it had not been signed by a celebrity, there were many within the story itself, and while I listed the film actresses, first ladies, grandes dames of the jet-set and the odd prince that the old guy had taken to bed, I heard commotion and guffawing in the audience. My output was by now copious, and the day before taking off for Turkey I had promised to give literary form to the Rio adventures of a German executive, who was now waiting for me in the agency. But I was feeling lazy, strolled slowly along the beachfront, looking at the girls on bikes, stopped to drink coconut water, almost fell asleep on the counter, and when I arrived the German had just left. I stood for a while in the reception area, unsure as to what to do, and Álvaro's piercing voice came through the walls: But the idea to hand out oranges was the governor's . . . but then all the horses'd have to be numbered . . . of course, no one gets herpes through the phone . . . OK, look, mate, if you want, I can come up with a rejoinder . . . then let's forget about it, bye . . . hi! . . . The receptionist wanted to let Álvaro know I was there, but I told her not to. I was over-whelmed by laziness, time zones, jetlag, the desire to go home.

I turned the key, no one in the living room, water running in the kitchen, the maid. I crossed the corridor, found the bedroom door closed, turned the door-knob silently. The afternoon sun was already setting, seeping through the blinds and projecting a kind of grid on the floor and bedspread. The bathroom was open, the light on. Wrapped in a white towel, her feet apart, Vanda threw her head forward, almost touching the ground, as if doing a kind of penance. She brushed

23

her brown hair forward from the nape of her neck, and I was able to observe her legs, arms, naked shoulders, the skin I knew to be equally brown all over her body, except on her breasts and under her knickers. Suddenly seeing Vanda like that at such close range, however, I was once again surprised. My first doubt, whenever I returned home from a trip, was whether Vanda became more exuberant in my absence, or faded in my thoughts. Her red face came up, she saw me in the mirror and wavered: Did you come through the balcony? No, I stole the key. You're crazy, my husband could turn up any minute. Your husband is in Istanbul. He can't be, I've been expecting him since yesterday! His plane went down. Oh! I took a step forward and leant against her. Barefoot, she barely reached my chin, and we stood staring at one another in the mirror for a good while, me squeezing her hips the way she liked me to. Until she softened and turned, her head hanging to the right, mouth half-open and lashes fluttering over closed eyes; after the kiss, when her lips left mine, she would say she was sleepy. Her lips left mine, she leant on the counter, facing me with her eyes still shut, rubbed them and said: I'm half asleep. She passed me like a sleepwalker, her steps slow but straight, and dropped on to the bed, inert, the white towel resting on her body. And the sun invaded the room, and the shadows of the blinds printed a cage over the towel on the body on the bed. Vanda pretended to be asleep, waiting for me to run my tongue behind her ear. I held back a few seconds on purpose, thinking the towel was a perfect mould for her body; if I carefully peeled it off her body, I could in theory construct another Vanda on her stomach beside her. Finally I knelt on the ground and ran my tongue behind her ear, which smelled of soap. Suddenly she sprang from the bed and I thought she was going to resume the husband game, but no. It was her mother's intuition sensing the boy downstairs in the playground or garage of the building, because just a few minutes later his cries came into the flat. Vanda was already at the bedroom door in a blouse and pair of jeans, What happened, what happened? Nothing had happened, a boy had hit the boy and the nanny had brought him home from school early. Sprawling across the bed, it was I who now pretended to be asleep, but I could see that the boy had gained a few pounds. My son was obese.

The German had no hair, not a shadow of a beard, nor eyebrows; he was perfectly glabrous. Although he was not old, the skin of his face was parched, probably the consequence of the Rio sun, seven summers of skin peeling away from skin peeling away from skin until arriving at this, skin a little like paper, a temporary husk that stuck around. He straightened up in his chair as soon as I turned on the recorder, and spoke exotic though fluent Portuguese, only interrupted by the changing of tapes, or when Álvaro came into the room. He would come in without knocking, Álvaro would, for no particular reason, go out, come back with a contract for the German to sign, go out, leave the door open. Even when there was no German, he kept coming in at any old time, saying any old thing and sneaking glances at my computer, forcing me to cover the screen with my hands to protect my drafts. Only late in the afternoon, when he and his lads left the agency, did I feel safe to get on with the job. I randomly picked one of the twenty cassette tapes the German had recorded, vaguely listened to his voice, rested my fingers on the keyboard, and I was a blond pink man seven years earlier, when I weighed anchor in Hamburg and entered Guanabara Bay. Of this city I knew nothing, nor did I intend to learn the native language; I had been sent to sort out the Company, and at the Company only German was spoken. I did not expect to meet Teresa, who introduced me to the Lusty Skunk, a corner bar where beer was drunk and sambas were sung all night long. There I became initiated in the tongue in which I presume to write this book in my own hand, which would have been un-imaginable seven years ago when I weighed anchor in Hamburg and entered Guanabara Bay. At first the

26

language, the climate, the food, the city, the people, everything, everything struck me as so absurd and hostile that I fell ill, and when I got out of bed days later, I saw in horror my naked body and my hair scattered across the sheet. Then I met Teresa and became acquainted with the country. I went to the corner bar, I went to the slum, I went to the football, but it took me a while to go to the beach because I was ashamed. I turned off the lights to sleep with Teresa, but she stroked my whole body, said I was sexy and soft as a snake. A dusky beauty like Teresa would have been unimaginable seven years ago when I weighed anchor in Hamburg. I would have married her in a chapel on an island in Guanabara Bay had she not traded me in for a Swiss cook, and that was when I went bald all over; I even lost my pubes, the hair from my armpits, everything, and the doctor's diagnosis was stress-induced alopecia. It was supposed to be a temporary baldness, but it wasn't, and I ended up getting used to my lack of hair, which I did not miss more than Teresa, and even without Teresa I ended up getting used to it. I forgot Teresa as I had already forgotten Hamburg, and left the Company to set up an NGO, or better, to pick up women on the beach, which would have been unimaginable seven years ago when I entered Guanabara Bay and, in ecstasy, lost all of my hair, but this text of mine was going around in circles, spinning its wheels, getting nowhere. Something was disturbing me, bizarre words sprang to mind, I flayed the skin of my fingers on the keyboard and at the end of the night threw it all away. I arrived home stumbling and found my place in the bed occupied by a fat child. In fact, I did not even touch on the subject with Vanda any more, because she always had an answer for everything. In addition to being enormous, the boy was about to turn five and still wasn't speaking. He said Mummy, Nanny, wee-wee, and Vanda said that Aristotle was mute until he was eight; God knows where she got that from. And he had developed the habit of babbling things incoherently in the middle of the night, inventing irritating sounds, clucking noises with the corners of his mouth. I had no peace even in my own bed; I tried to contain myself, bit my tongue and finally exploded: Shut up, for God's sake! He did, and Vanda came out in his defence: He's just imitating you. Imitating what? Imitating you, now that you've taken to talking in your sleep. Me? You. Me? You. Since when? Since you got back from that trip. There. At that instant I discovered I spoke Hungarian in my dreams.

My passage through Budapest had dissipated in my brain. When I remembered it, it was like a quick accident, a wobbly frame in the film of memory. An

28

illusory episode, perhaps, which I didn't go to the trouble of explaining to Vanda or anyone else. Nor was Vanda interested, in all honesty, in knowing who these great writers were that I met with every year at conferences that never made the news. Perhaps she was avoiding fantasising about her husband's adventures through the world, poetesses, editresses, women of letters that made me lose my better judgement and return flight. As such, it would be silly to recount, without conviction, my solitary night in Budapest to a Vanda that did not want to hear it. And this Budapest would have been dead and buried by now, had the boy not raised it from my dreams. An attempt to get closer to his father, I was soon to understand, which I had repudiated with inexplicable brutality. At six-thirty on the dot in the mornings to come, when mother and son were woken by the alarm clock, I also forced myself to rise. I began to dedicate my spare time before work, normally spent lounging around, meditating on life and reading newspapers on the toilet, to the boy. Now, when Vanda left for the studio, I stayed in the kitchen having breakfast with my son. Watching him with ice-creams and Cokes, I tried to retrieve the lost features in his flaccid face, and admitted that they were those of a beautiful boy. With the tip of a napkin, I cleaned the frosted flakes from his mouth and found his mother's fleshy lips, just as his black eyes were his mother's. I was about to brush aside the brown curls hanging over his cheeks but, self-conscious, caught myself in time; in my hands was the gesture that caressed Vanda's cheeks. For over a month I waited for him to repeat the words from my dream, as only in this manner would I feel redeemed. Speak, my son, I almost begged, grasping his wrists, but at this point he would burst into tears, calling for Mummy, calling for Nanny. And at least the nanny shared my distress about the boy's aphasia. She said that when she was new on the job she had warned Vanda: babies that see their reflections in the mirror end up tongue-tied. Vanda did not laugh when I mentioned this, and assured me that when I wasn't around the boy was making con-siderable progress. Possessive, she meant that my constant assistance might suffocate him. As a precau-tion, I went back to lolling about in bed until later. The thought of the Hungarian words, however, kept coming back to torment me in bed, in the bathroom and above all in the agency, facing the computer, its empty screen the colour of ice. And it so happened that one day Álvaro invaded my little room shaking a newspaper: Check this out, your gringo's turning into a star. A cultural column stated that the Rio-based businessman Kaspar Krabbe was giving the finishing touches to his memoirs written in the form of a novel. I was startled, and thought about calling the German; I needed to let him know that the job was a little behind schedule, but my eyes slid to another notice at the foot of the page: A reception will be held tonight at the Hungarian Consulate in honour of the distinguished poet Kocsis Ferenc.

I could never be bothered dining out, no one invited me to parties, the theatre got on my nerves and I waited for new films to come out on video, which is why Vanda was barely concerned with where we were going when I called her from the agency; she got the maid to press my grey suit and took off for the shopping centre. These days, she went around the house in T-shirts, shorts and jeans, perhaps the wardrobe of a woman resigned to her lot, but which in my eyes had already become her signature label. Even presenting the news, she wore casual, homely clothes. It was no wonder then that the boy got a fright when she emerged in a black skirt and jacket, stilettos, necklaces, earrings, blusher and lipstick, her hair in a bun with the ends fastened down in curls. To calm her son and get him to sleep she had to undress, wash her face, undo her hair, and it took her another hour and a half to do herself up again and meet me in the garage. On the way to Flamengo Beach I improvised praise for Kocsis Ferenc, the great interpreter of the Hungarian soul, and cited *Secret Tercets* as his most famous work. I had made them up on the spot, these tercets, but Vanda was quick to say she had heard of them, having read about them in a literary supplement. She added that Ferenc's book had received many awards, been launched in scores of countries, even translated into Chinese, and it was a pleasure to hear her rabbiting on like that. I laughed inwardly; I always got my own back for liking Vanda. She was still going on about *Secret Tercets* when we arrived at the Consulate and found no photographers, no security guards, no cars with diplomatic licence plates, no valet parking, no one at all; in front of the building was a lamppost, two tiny palms and the space where I parked my car. A night watchman opened the iron gate for us without asking a thing, and when I pressed the lift button I noticed a slight tremor in my hand. When we arrived at the sixth floor, Vanda and I looked at one another; I had prepared my spirit for the language of Budapest more or less in the same way that she was dripping with jewellery. And we found ourselves there in a silent little lift foyer, lit only by a crack in the door of flat 602. But as soon as I dared push the door open, the Consulate burst into applause. Then the fifty or so people standing around the room, facing the window, relaxed, came to life, turned round and began to talk to one another. It was the sound of the Hungarian language that enveloped me as I penetrated the room. The Hungarian voices trilled around me, never suspecting that they were revealing their secrets to an intruder. And ignorant of their meanings, I heard the inflections of the language more clearly; I was alert to every ellipsis, every hesitation, interrupted sentence, words split down the middle like fruit I could peer inside. Engrossed in the centre of the party, I was slow to remember Vanda, who I had abandoned at the door. And there she remained, entertained by a circle of ladies who probably recognised her from the television. I drew closer to see what she found so amusing, but it was also in Hungarian that they told her things with which she agreed by nodding her head. Vanda was truly an attraction in a room full of middle-aged people, all somewhat alike, dressed with similar simplicity, in a family-birthday-like atmosphere. A gentleman wearing a grey suit exactly like mine, perhaps the Consul himself, went around the room with a diamond-cut crystal decanter, serving the guests. When he happened upon Vanda and me empty-handed, he hurried to fetch two glasses of very sweet liqueur, tasting of apricot. He was followed by a woman with purplish hair holding a tray of bread rolls. The pumpkin rolls, I thought, but she did a half-turn and, following her example, everyone fell silent and turned to face the window again. A tall, slightly stooped man stood there, appearing younger than he appeared, because he had the appearance of a young man with the air of an old man. The breeze tugged at his very fine hair, and Sugarloaf was lit in the background, pumpkin-coloured. It could only have been Kocsis Ferenc, a book in one hand, a glass in the other. I moved in closer to the poet, pulling Vanda with me, as he spoke quietly in a deep, husky voice. He recited a poem known to the audience, who whispered the refrain in unison with him: *Egyetlen, érintetlen, lefordíthatatlan.* Smiling, Vanda stretched up to my ear and I did not believe she would dare translate those lines. Joaquim, was what she whispered, because, when he emitted those three words, the poet made a light clucking noise with the back of his tongue, just like our son when he imitated me. The poem gained intensity along with the strength of the wind coming through the window, which mussed up the poet's hair and the pages of his book. But Kocsis Ferenc no longer consulted the book in order to recite heart-rending rhymes; his blue eyes sought the eyes of each spectator, including mine. His bloodshot blue eyes finally fixed on my wife's black eyes. He paused, downed his liqueur in a single gulp and resumed his recital without taking his eyes off my wife. I watched her obliquely, her mouth half-open, eyelashes tremulous, blood rising to her face, and there was a tear in her left eye when the fellow finished with a flourish: *Egyetlen, érintetlen, lefordíthatatlan!* Applause broke out, then everyone relaxed, came to life and turned round, except Vanda, who, gazing at the Hungarian, looked like a saint gazing upwards in prayer, hands still clasped from her last clap. I had to shake her, then pulled her across the room by the arm and slipped out the door without saying goodbye. Driving along Botafogo Beach, Vanda insinuated that I had had a fit of jealousy, but she was the only one who had not noticed that the poet was gay. In Copacabana I asked if she wanted to stop off for Japanese and she grew thoughtful. It was raining in Ipanema and with her hand on my thigh she told me there was pea soup at home. I kissed her on the lips in the garage, she softened, pretended to be asleep on her feet in the lift, and off we went.

In the mornings, without Vanda around, I could have met with clients in a corner of the living room and got on with my work without intrusions. It occurred to me several times to lug my computer and dictionaries home, although that may have been all Álvaro needed to remove me from the partnership. He had already considerably reduced my share in the company, understandably perhaps: he shouldn't have to pay the wages of ten writers who, all said and done, performed tasks that were my responsibility. But with five per cent of Cunha & Costa, he said, I could live in the lap of luxury, lunch in Paris and dine in New York, go diving in the Caribbean with my wife and travel around the world until I was dizzy. And it was precisely about my next vacation with Vanda that I was thinking the day Álvaro burst into the room holding a cordless phone, speaking louder than usual. It was the first time I had seen a mobile phone, and in my distraction I almost forgot to cover the monitor. But between my fingers he must have caught sight of a heart, diamonds, a king, an eight of spades, the green background; for some time now I had only been turning on the computer to play patience. He was on the line with the German and apologised on my behalf for the word given, the deadline broken, the advance squandered overseas, the insignificant contractual fine. He hung up and said that, if I didn't mind, he was going to outsource the German's book, since he had just hired a lad who was a genius, and I don't know if he was bluffing or really did intend to put me down. At any rate, I shut down the game that very instant, rolled up my sleeves, rested my fingers on the keyboard, weighed anchor in Hamburg, entered Guanabara Bay and I chose not to listen to the German's tapes. I was a healthy young blond man when I entered Guanabara Bay, roved the streets of Rio de Janeiro and met Teresa. When I heard Teresa sing, I fell in love with her language, and after three months of vacillation, I felt that the German's story was at my fingertips. The writing flowed spontaneously, at a pace that was not mine, and it was on Teresa's calf that I wrote my first words in the local tongue. At first she kind of liked it and was flattered when I told her I was writing a book on her. Later she took it into her head to get jealous, to refuse me her body, saying I only wanted her to write on, and the book was already in the vicinity of chapter seven when she abandoned me. Without her, I lost the plot, returned to the preface, my knowledge of the language receded, and I even thought about giving it all up and returning to Hamburg. I spent my days catatonic before a blank sheet of paper: I had become addicted to Teresa. I tried writing something on myself, but it wasn't as good, so I went to Copacabana in search of whores. I paid to write on them, and perhaps paid more than I should have, as they simulated orgasms that robbed me of all concentration. I rang the bell at Teresa's house, she was married, I cried, she gave me her hand and allowed me to write a few brief words while her husband was out. I began to besiege schoolgirls, who sometimes allowed me to write on their blouses, then in the folds of their arms, where they were ticklish, then on their skirts, thighs. And they showed this writing to their peers, who greatly admired it, and they came to my flat and asked me to write my book on their faces, their necks, then they removed their blouses and offered me their breasts, tummies and backs. And they showed my writing to other peers, who came to my flat and begged me to rip off their knickers, and the black of my letters shone against their blushing buttocks. Girls came and went from my life, and my book became scattered, each chapter taking off in a different direction. That was when I met the one who lay on my bed and taught me to write back to front. Possessive of my writing, only she knew how to read it, looking at herself in the mirror, and she erased by night what had been written by day so that I would never cease writing my book on her. And she fell pregnant by me, and on her belly the book took on new forms, and I worked for days and nights on end, without eating a single sandwich, locked in the little room in the agency, until I composed, on my last legs, the final sentence: And my beloved, of whose milk I had partaken, made me drink from the water in which she had washed her blouse. I returned to the beginning of the text on the computer, and the revision of a book was a time of intense bonding for me. Before long it would have a new author, and relinquishing a book that was finished and ready was always painful, even for a seasoned professional like myself. But perhaps because it had gushed on to the page like that, I was unable to enjoy the German's book; the words slipped away from me. Recently written words, with the same speed with which they had been written, ceased to belong to me. I saw my words scattered across the screen and, in horror, imagined they were abandoning me as the German had lost his hair. I printed out the book, leafed through it for the last time, and feeling that it was my last one, suddenly didn't want to sell it for any price. I even went as far as to put the originals in a drawer and lock it, then I imagined Álvaro's face and opened the drawer. I shoved the bundle of papers into a brown envelope, handwrote the title *The Gynographer* on the label, and the letters were faint: it was as if my own ink was running out. I crossed the lads' office and their silence was so great that I thought I heard the sound of eyes following me. I entered Álvaro's office without knocking and tossed the envelope with the two-hundred-page book on his desk, but he was on the phone and paid little attention. I went downstairs to Avenida Atlântica; it was raining, the beach was deserted, the waters dark and choppy. I sought shelter in a kiosk and wondered if I would ever be able to live far from the sea, in a city that did not end abruptly like that, but agonised out in all directions. After staring for a time at the waves breaking and the waterline creeping up the sand, I felt my body sink forward slightly; it was as if the continent was tilting instead of the tide rising. I lost myself in the neighbourhood, went quickly into a chemist's and greeted the shop assistant, but left without knowing why I had entered. I ordered a beer in a corner bar, saw a travel agent's on the other side of the road, abandoned the beer, crossed the road and bought two tickets to Budapest.

Vanda brought the boy to the lift to convince him that I was leaving alone, with five large suitcases and two pieces of hand luggage. Sitting in the taxi, I waited the forty minutes that she needed to finish tricking the child into bed. We drove in silence to the airport, where the clerk asked for her autograph and allowed the excess baggage. In the VIP lounge, I ordered two glasses of champagne, we said cheers and nothing else. When the loudspeaker announced the flight to London, I believe I saw a slight contraction in Vanda's lips, but she got up quickly, gave me a kiss on the head and disappeared pulling her suitcase on wheels. I ordered another glass of champagne and flicked through a magazine full of faces that seemed out of focus. I still had a vivid image in my mind of Vanda's expression when she opened the ticket I had presented to her in a suede wallet, wrapped in tissue paper: Budapest? And what is there to do in Budapest? It was hard to answer: Look at the Danube? Drink liqueurs? Listen to poets? Vanda wanted to brush up her English, watch musicals, besides which her twin sister, Vanessa, was in London, and the two of them could traipse around Soho, play tennis, she didn't know anyone in Budapest, were there department stores in Budapest? Don't know, there must be confectioners, excellent museums. Budapest? No way! She went to the agency and changed her ticket, as one zips off to a boutique to exchange a present that's the wrong size. I might even have felt hurt, but there wasn't time; she felt hurt before me and said it was the first time I had refused to spend her holidays with her since our honeymoon. She didn't speak to me for days and nights, trying to make me feel remorse for her own attitude. And now, as I heard the last call for Paris, my connection, I felt a little sorry for Vanda, who, flying alone over the Atlantic Ocean, was perhaps reflecting on how unfair she had been. Perhaps at that moment she was mortified for not being with me, holding hands, taking off for Budapest. She could not have known that, deep down, I don't think I would have invited her to Budapest, had I not been sure I would fly alone.

I had never seen

KRISKA STRIPPED UNEXPECTEDLY, and I had never seen a body so white in my life. Her skin was so white all over that I was unsure how to touch her, where to park my hands. White, white, white, I said, beautiful, beautiful, beautiful; my vocabulary was poor. After gazing at her for a time, I wished only to stroke her breasts, her tiny pink nipples, but I still had not learnt to ask for things. I did not dare make a single move without her consent, Kriska being a lover of discipline. In our first lessons she made me go thirsty, because I said water, water, water, water, without getting the prosody right. As for the pumpkin rolls, one day she brought a steaming batch into the living room, waved them under my nose and threw them all away because I was unable to name them. But before memorising and learning to pronounce the words in a language correctly, we do begin to distinguish between them, grasp their meanings: table, coffee, telephone, forgetful, yellow, sigh, spaghetti Bolognese, window, shuttlecock, happiness, one, two, three, nine, ten, music, wine, cotton dress, tickles, bonkers, and one day I discovered that Kriska liked to be kissed on the neck. Then she pulled her oversized dress over her head; she had nothing on underneath, and I was disorientated by so much whiteness. For a second I imagined that she was not a woman who one could touch here or there, but who defied me to touch all of her skin at once. I even feared that at that very second she would say: Take me, make love to me, shag me, fuck me, ravage me; how is it that Hungarian women say these things? But she remained quiet, her gaze lost, moved, perhaps by my gaze wandering over her body, or my halting speech in her language, white, beautiful, beautiful, white, white, beautiful, white. And I was also moved, knowing that soon I would know her intimate parts and, with equal or greater pleasure, their names.

Kriska's nocturnal lessons sometimes went on into the small hours, and I would go straight from her house to the hotel. Often, on the way to the hotel, or even in the middle of the lesson, or when I awoke, or instead of sleeping, I wondered what Vanda was doing at that time in London. I knew she was the kind of woman who got up early to go sightseeing, made friends, filmed statues, ate lunch standing up, waited in queues, climbed stairs; when we travelled together we usually only met up at dinnertime. I can't really criticise her; I myself have seen so many cities superficially that now I might easily confuse them all. It took me a long time to learn that to know a city it is better to shut yourself away in a room within it than ride around it in a double-decker bus. It is not easy, and I knew that entering Budapest would not be easy. At the airport I had to resist the conveniences on offer to newcomers, the travel-agency girls, the taxis awaiting me with open doors: sir, *signor*, *monsieur*, mister. I entrusted my suitcase to a more discreet professional and we waited a minute in silence in the car. I finally ventured a Plaza Hotel. It was what occurred to me, because there is a hotel with this name in every city in the world. *Yo yo*, the driver said, and drove me through some blurred neighbourhoods, their mercury-vapour streetlamps few and far between. I was very tired, my eyes were smarting, I dozed off, and suddenly we were driving through a city so brightly lit that one did not see its façades, corners and spaces, only its lights. One of these signs belonged to the Plaza Hotel, which, like most Plaza hotels, was not situated on a square at all, but a steep street. Sorry, *désolé*, they couldn't find my reservation but I feigned ignorance, continued drumming on the counter, and they ended up putting me in a room with a balcony. I went outside, and found the street was full of typical restaurants and clubs: *buona sera, bienvenue*, the real goulash, the crazy czardas, *se habla español*, etc. I strolled up the street, and it took on the air of a residential neighbourhood, leafy, calm, with two-storey stone houses built in the nineteenth century. I was already seven blocks up when I heard some wails, like the moans of a hoarse woman and a wounded man, and I thought I saw a couple entangled behind a poplar. I stopped, thinking it best to head back down to the hotel, but a blonde girl detached herself from the tree and addressed me. She seemed to be asking for something, a cigarette maybe, and being approached in Hungarian went to my head, made me feel truly honoured. I had no cigarettes as I had given up smoking a year before, but without thinking, I answered: *Yo yo*. The blonde swung round, making her short skirt flutter, and with great excitement said something to the tree, from where a young man with strong arms emerged, wearing no shirt and a khaki vest full of pockets, the sort photographers wear. With a wave of her arm and a jerk of his head, they gestured for me to accompany them along a side street to the left. I followed them, a little concerned that I might lose my bearings as we left the street of the hotel. But our destination was a hundred yards ahead, a small house with a purple neon sign that looked like handwriting: The Arsehole.

A bar with an English name, furnished like an English pub, with speakers playing English rock and roll; I imagined that The Arsehole was patronised exclusively by Hungarians. But in its half-darkness the young clientele did not snub me, neither for being a foreigner, nor for being almost forty with thinning hair. We sat at a minuscule round table, the blonde in the short pink skirt who looked underage, her photographer boyfriend, thirty at the most, and I. A waitress appeared without being called, exchanged three little kisses with each of them and served three glasses of firewater. She stood next to me swinging a bag of coins, her naked thigh with cellulite wedged against the edge of the table, and I understood then that I had been invited to finance a night of carousing in the bar. I willingly forked out my forints, paying for this and another ten or twelve rounds of the firewater that I was unable to identify, as it was too cold and smelled of pure alcohol. A few cans of beer also arrived, which the blonde drank, dancing between the tables, bumping into the tables, falling into people's laps. Not satisfied, she began to gyrate in front of me, while her boyfriend smoked a cigar, looking at the ceiling, and everyone made comments at the top of their lungs because of the volume of the music. The blonde was insolent and pointed at me in fits of laughter, shouting at the photographer: I'll get this good-time guy in bed with me, or: With me this guy'll get it good at bedtime, or: It's time I got this guy's goods into bed, or something of the sort. I already considered myself on the verge of mastering Hungarian, when spoken loudly and clearly. This guy in bed could be your stepfather, was what I understood the photographer to say, after twisting his mouth and pointing at me with his chin. He then stubbed out the cigar with his boot, got up, stood in front of her and he was double her size; he could have knocked her down with a light cuff. He grabbed her by the hips, threw her up in the air, caught her with just one arm, set her spinning across the room, red knickers on display, then leapt on to the table, crossed his legs and flung them open in the air in a horizontal line. An elastic sort, his boot narrowly missed the waitress's ponytail and the entire bar clapped along with the rhythm of the rock and roll. The blonde tried to copy him clumsily, the crowd found it funny, and I judged it time to leave. I missed my step as I got up and lunged headlong at the door, as my torso was faster than my legs. I inhaled the night air, took off to the right, hesitated, returned, and there was the couple again, waving at me from the front of The Arsehole.

They offered to show me the way back, *yo yo*, I really was in need of some orientation. They walked ahead of me, the girl like a child hanging from his arm, and seeing that scene moved me, reminded me of a film I can't recall. They stopped beside a tree. It was the poplar where I had found them, and I took my leave with a discreet wave, thinking they wanted to be left to their own devices again. But they drew up alongside me further down the street in an unnecessary gesture of courtesy, as I already knew I was seven blocks from the hotel. They followed me into the hotel, hung back in the lobby while I collected my key and caught up with me in the lift. I had barely opened the door when the photographer settled on to my bed and lit a narrow pipe. And the blonde led me to the balcony, from where one could see Budapest from one end to the other. A cloudy day was breaking and the city was grey; it's funny, I had imagined Budapest as being yellow, but it was completely grey, the buildings, the parks, even the Danube that cut through it in a Y, forking off in the distance. The blonde took my hand, studied it, sighed, traced my palm with a fingernail and sighed. She then pressed it to her chest for me to feel her heart pounding. And by the hand she led me back into the bedroom, where I saw the photographer with his head down, sitting on the edge of the bed, moving his wrist back and forth. I thought it unpleasant of him to masturbate on my bed, but no, it was the chamber of a revolver that he was spinning between his legs. He pointed me to a chair in front of

49

him, while the blonde sat on the ground, her legs folded under her. On the bedside table were five bullets, which he put one by one into a vest pocket, counting from one to five with meticulous diction, *unu*, *doi*, *trei*, *patru*, *chinch*. He looked at the ceiling, whistled a tune, suddenly raised the revolver to his left ear as if answering an urgent telephone call. He made a face, she tensed her shoulders, he pulled the trigger, there was a click. He cleared his throat, laid the gun on the ground and a long silence ensued; there were no birds in Budapest, not even a cock in the distance, a dog. I decided to laugh but my laughter had a metallic ring. The blonde picked up the revolver by the butt, she was also left-handed, and crossed herself with her right hand. She stuck the barrel in her ear, the revolver was enormous in her hand, I didn't think her forefinger would reach the trigger, it did. She even wiggled the barrel into her ear as if trying to find the deepest fit, the shortest path for the bullet, fired, and nothing, click. She looked me between the eyes with the slightest of squints, laid the revolver in my hand, it was the first time I had held a firearm. I opened my mouth, the blonde winked at me, I stuck the barrel against the roof of my mouth, I was unafraid. I pulled the trigger and only after the click did the fear come, the barrel began to rattle between my teeth, the butt stuck in my hand, my hand stiffened, I rested the

50

revolver on the bedside table but was unable to let go and it clattered like castanets on the wood. My hand finally went limp, all the muscles of my body relaxed, I felt the weariness of the night, plus the previous night in the plane, plus the nights before that in bed with Vanda, the boy kicking me. My eyelids gave in, I felt all my nights of insomnia weighing down on one another.

I opened my eyes with a start and saw the photographer with the revolver back in his hand, which was shaking; for an instant I believed it was not his hand, but the revolver still shaking from my shudder. He lifted it to his head, lowered it again, examined it, shook it, abandoned it on the carpet, and I was happy with this, the drinking binge and show of bravado was over. I was about to give him a hug, kiss the blonde's hand, see them to the door, fill his pockets with little bottles from the mini fridge, when I saw him pushing the revolver towards me with the tip of his boot. He must have discovered that I didn't speak Hungarian, because he emphatically repeated some circular gestures. He was trying to tell me that the Russian roulette had gone clockwise and now the direction should be reversed, starting with me. He was cheating, making up a ridiculous rule, I wanted to protest, but didn't even know how to say no in Hungarian. I was saved by the blonde, who took the revolver, tried to shove it back into her

51

boyfriend's hand, and then he called her a cow. He practically spelled it out: $V - a - c - a$, as we Latins have said cow since ancient Rome, and I came to the conclusion that the impostor didn't speak Hungarian either. He was Romanian, with a bronze medallion around his neck, a hoop earring at his ear, a ring on each finger. He was a Romanian gypsy, and the blonde was right when she said: I am disgusted by your grotesque spectacle, at least that's what I heard. And to humiliate him, she turned the gun to her own forehead and fired, without blinking. There was no bullet, it served him right, now the gypsy had no choice; he picked up the revolver, pointed it at his temple and I calculated that, when the blast shattered his bones, his brains would splatter on the blonde's hair, it would be revolting. It would be sickening, but I couldn't stop looking, and I saw how his finger joints closed on the trigger, I even heard the spring grating in the trigger, and click. Nothing, he didn't die, tossed the revolver into my lap, showed the blonde his gold teeth, then they both turned to face me. And it was thus evident that through some ruse, some gypsy sleight of hand, they had reserved the bullet in the cylinder for me. They were after my money, from the start, they had been organising my death. And it would be a death as opportune for them as it was inglorious for me, the suicide of an inebriated tourist in Budapest.

I stood, levelling the gun at them, and walked backwards, as I could not turn my back on such sinister lowlifes. They both rose at the same time, herded me around the room, and while on the one hand he had muscles, fists and sharp rings, on the other, her face was more murderous. Her jaw undershot, she walked erect and flared her nostrils with the inverse arrogance of the short, and although I aimed straight in their faces, they did not drop their pace. That was when I began to doubt that the game had been for real because nobody walks unprotected towards a loaded gun, except in the movies. And when I found my heels against the wall I shoved the barrel into my mouth, forcing them to respect me. They braked a short distance away and now time was mine; I was in the position of a performer. I turned the revolver to my ear, my heart, from one eye to the other, ran the barrel around my mouth like lipstick, and swallowed it again, determined to put an end to the game. I cocked the hammer, she tensed her shoulders, he made a face, then I tasted something strange. I tasted lead in the gun, it was already releasing lead on my tongue, and now it was too late, I could not stop. All I could do was squeeze the trigger little by little, in the hope that the bullet might come out slowly, but in the meantime someone knocked at the door of the room. There was commotion in the corridor, shouting, doors slamming, the footsteps of heavy people. The gypsies backed away and I took the opportunity to throw the revolver against the opposite wall, to see if the impact would trigger it off. But what was heard was a pealing of bells over our heads; all the bells in Budapest had begun to chime. I opened the door, found a bunch of Danes in Bermuda shorts going past and joined them. I forcefully squeezed into the crowded lift and on the ground floor I ran into the gypsies charging down the last flight of stairs. I pretended not to know them and headed for the pavement outside the hotel, where more Danes were assembling next to a bus and a tour guide was handing out pamphlets. I already had one foot in the bus when I saw the couple moving away up the street, the girl hanging from his arm, limping slightly.

I pulled out of the excursion, went up to my room, stretched out on the bed and opened the pamphlet, which was an illustrated map of the city, with white streets on a beige background, green-hued gardens and a blue Danube. On the eastern bank, Pest, on the western, Buda, where the Plaza Hotel was marked with a red arrow. It did not show street names and the street where the hotel was located was a long straight line that came up from the river and ran off the map. If I took a cross street, I was three fingers from the historical centre of Buda, an irregular arrangement of streets accompanied by other arrows, and circles in various colours, and crosses representing churches, and asterisks referring to an index with explanations in English. But I was not looking for explanations; I intended to allow my eyes to wander slowly through that urban design. And throughout the day I scrutinised streets and alleys of Buda, strode along the top of its city wall, passed through the walls of the medieval castle. Strolling around a map like that did not bother me, perhaps because I have always had the vague feeling that I was also the map of a person. I only set aside my pastime to see some men bellowing at one another on television, in a political debate which, although dead on my feet, I watched to the end, without sound. I had muted the sound shortly after turning on the TV, as listening to such a strange language was beginning to disturb me. I thought the language would invade my weary head while I slept, thought I would catch myself speaking a strange language when I awoke. I imagined that the following day I would go out into the strange city speaking a language that everyone understood, except me. It grew late, I switched the TV off and on, turned the sound up and down, flicked the lamp off and on, sent for pillows, sandwiches and, when I saw the news-reader opening and closing her mouth on the three o'clock news, I remembered Vanda. I called the

London Plaza, thinking she might be sprawling on her bed like me, eating a ham and cheese sandwich, watching the BBC news. I would have loved to hear her talking nonsense about the latest events, as she knew little more English than I did Hungarian. But it was just as well I didn't find her; Vanda would know I was calling for nothing, calling merely to hear her voice. Even so, I soon rang again, but it was in vain; she must have gone out with her sister. I left my name and number with the telephonist, thought about my wife a little longer, thought I would never sleep again in my entire life, and swallowed a sleeping pill. I was woken by the light in the room, the bells chiming six, the television showing the news, and it took me some time to place the mute newsreader plastered with pancake, all those fluffy pillows, and I wasn't sure if I'd slept three hours or twenty-seven. I called Vanda again, but she still hadn't arrived at the hotel, which in a way was a blessing; if she had detected any indecision in my voice, she would certainly have gloated: Budapest . . . didn't I say so?

I went to the window, gazed across the city and went back to bed; I could easily have slept until the following day. Then I remembered the map and found the red arrow pointing at the hotel; I was one palm from the other side of the river. Judging from the amount of arrows, crosses, asterisks, yellow circles and blue triangles, I figured that Pest was livelier than Buda. The major hotels and restaurants were there, as well as theatres, cinemas, boutiques, shopping centres, and on a bustling street of shops I noticed a series of little green planes, which, according to the index, represented airlines. I would have to book my return flight at some stage, as my ticket was open. If I paid a small difference, I could definitely extend it, spend a weekend in London, for example. I could even leave that night, if it were possible, seeing as I already knew Buda like the back of my hand and had a whole day for Pest. I sprang out of bed, went down the stairs, found a dazzling day outside and a bus gushing Danes into the hotel. I arrived at the Danube so quickly that I looked at my feet to be sure I was walking with them and not my thoughts. I watched a few minutes of Danube go past, moss-green and much wider than it looked on the map. I jogged across the chain bridge, found myself in a large square with a statue in the middle, quickly admired the neoclassical façades, the art nouveau balconies, the Byzantine arches, on the third corner breathed in tobacco, chocolate, onion, turned right, passed in front of Kodak, Benetton, C&A, cut through an arcade, turned left, Lufthansa, American Airlines, Alitalia, the Air France agency was still closed. I positioned myself in front of the door to ensure I would be served first, and people passed back and forth behind me speaking jumbled sentences. I waited and waited, it grew dark, then I realised I had woken at six in the evening. I tried to reconstruct my itinerary in reverse, but became confused by the lights of bars, discos and pizzerias that hadn't been there on my way in. It started raining, taxis went past full, I found an open bookshop and went inside; if I was to leave the country the following day without managing to string two words together, I would take a dictionary as a souvenir. I found a shelf replete with thick volumes, ran my eyes across the Hungarian titles on their spines and my impression was that of a truly disorganised, chaotic library. Then I looked more closely and saw that the covers were all aligned; it was the letters that looked out of order. That is why my eyes were drawn to the book that was the most modest, but with a legible title: *Hungarian in 100 Lessons*. Leafing through it, I caught glimpses of conversation exercises: Does this train go to Bulgaria? My wife is vegetarian. How tall is the old obelisk? I need to buy cheap candlesticks. Where does that soldier live? Then I noticed the tall woman with a backpack looking at the book in my hands and shaking her head. I thought she was a store detective and that handling the merchandise was forbidden. I immediately held out the book, which she seized and flung any old how on to the bottom of a shelf. I presumed the harshness of the gesture to be characteristic of the Huns, like her cheekbones, somewhat prominent, or her lips that I thought cruel for their lack of flesh. And when she stated that one does not learn the Magyar language from books, I was astonished, because the sentence sounded perfectly intelligible to me. I even wondered if she had spoken in Portuguese, or English, or perhaps Romanian, but it was indeed Hungarian, because I was unable to distinguish a single word. Nonetheless I was left with no doubt: she had stated that one does not learn the Magyar language from books. Perhaps she had a way of singing the language, which, although I couldn't understand it, I picked up by ear. Perhaps I was able to understand what she meant through her intonation alone. Or perhaps because I understood the music, guessing the lyrics seemed easy to me. I thus expected new words, but she sprang into motion and literally darted away like an arrow, her head flying over the centre shelves of the bookshop. She left, stopped short under the shop awning to watch the end of the rain, and only when I caught up with her did I notice she was wearing skates. I positioned myself beside her and, unsure as to how to express myself, casually took the map from my pocket and murmured: Plaza Hotel. She wrenched it from my hand, and I thought she would throw it in the gutter, as one did not learn Budapest from maps either. But she opened it, analysed it:

Plaza . . . Plaza . . . Plaza . . . Plaza . . . *yo*. And on the way to the hotel I had my first peripatetic Hungarian lesson, which consisted of her naming the things I pointed at: street, skates, drop of water, puddle, night, pizzeria, disco, bar, arcade, shop window, clothes, photograph, corner, grocer's, bonbon, tobacconist's, Byzantine arch, art *nouveau* balcony, neoclassical façade, statue, square, chain bridge, river, moss-green, steep street, reception, lobby, coffee shop, mineral water and Kriska.

Kriska chattered along the way, her marching skates clattering on the pavement, signs and headlights flashing in her face, but no sooner had we sat in the flat light of the hotel coffee shop than she lit a cigarette and fell silent. It was no wonder; it was such an empty, stark setting that after pointing at the bare walls, the glass table, the metal chair, the waiter in white, the bottle, the glass, the ashtray, the lighter, the flame and the Fecske brand cigarette, *fecske* being the swallow printed on the packet, I ran out of topics. And we remained like that for a good half-hour, staring at the ash in the ashtray, because I had no way of pointing at the things that passed through my head: my wife in London, the girls on skates in Ipanema, my partner's weedy laugh, the blue eyes of my client with no eyelashes, the man who wrote on women, the anonymous writers in Istanbul, the girls on skates in Ipanema, my wife in London. But two people do not remain in equilibrium for very long side by side, each with their own silence. One of the silences ends up sucking in the other, and that was when I turned to face Kriska, who paid me no heed. I observed her silence, certainly deeper than mine and somehow more silent. And we stayed like that for another half an hour, she inside herself and I immersed in her silence, trying to read her thoughts quickly before they became Hungarian words. Then she shook all over, as if gripped by a chill, making her backpack slide down her back, and looked for a calling card, which she scrawled on in pencil and handed to me. And she got up and left without saying goodbye, gliding across the carpet on her skates. I think I had grown fond of that silence, and in order to prolong it I retired to my room, where I spent the rest of the night staring at the ceiling. I felt a little hungry, but I didn't call room service; I also thought a little about Vanda, but I didn't call London. When I heard the morning bells, doors banging, trays toppling, glass shattering and chambermaids arguing in the corridor, I fell asleep. And I slept for twelve hours straight, because now I had a simple thought. My thought was a calling card on the bedside table, with her name printed on it: Fülemüle Krisztina, and her address, Tóth utca, 84, 17, Újpest, plus the class time she had jotted down,

61

8–10 p.m., and an amount, 3,000 forints, which seemed a reasonable daily rate.

Well ahead of time I took a taxi, which left me at 84 Tóth Street in twenty minutes. I stood in front of the electronic gate for another forty before announcing myself on the intercom: José Costa. It was a private cul-de-sac of terraced houses, and Kriska was waiting for me on the doorstep of number 17; without her skates, she was almost small and less girlish. She said Zsoze Kósta . . . Zsoze Kósta . . . looking me up and down as if my name were inappropriate attire. I let her say Zsoze Kósta until she got used to it and did not correct her pronunciation, nor did I make fun of Kriska, rather, I concurred with her and came to be known as Zsoze Kósta in Budapest. She soon abandoned the Zsoze and called me Kósta, believing this to be my Christian name, which comes after the surname for Hungarians. And she made me call her Kriska, like all Hungarian Christines; Kriska and nothing else. I think we dispensed with certain formalities right at the outset due to the fact that I visited her early in the evening, catching them in a state of disorder, her and the house. To make space for us on the study table, she would often pile up the tablecloth and that night's dinner dishes in the opposite corner. She would also quickly pull her hair up on top of her head with an elastic band, and just as a few strands would fall across her face, there were always a few leftover crumbs on the table. Not to mention that every other day her son prowled around, fiddling with things, laughing at me, and he would not settle until Kriska sent him to bed. He thought it funny, Pisti did, to see a grown man looking at pictures in colourful albums, a stuttering man learning to say umbrella, cage, ear, bicycle. *Kêrekport, kêrekpart, kerékpár,* Kriska made me repeat each word a thousand times over, syllable by syllable, but my efforts to imitate her resulted at most in a feminine, rather than Hungarian, mode of speech. And no one could blame her for losing her patience, biting her tongue, spilling her coffee, lighting the filter of her cigarettes; this was not lost on me. In the first few days I was truly convinced that, in addition to taking up smoking again, I would absorb nothing from her lessons. The classes exhausted me and after two hours my forehead throbbed, but not even this made me want to return to the hotel. Nor did Kriska hurry me along; after putting away the albums in her backpack, she would serve me a glass of apricot liqueur and go about her domestic chores as if I did not exist, or was a member of the household, which is much the same. She would take the dishes into the kitchen, turn on the dishwasher, shake the tablecloth out the window, pace around the living room, her head to one side, the cordless phone pressed against her shoulder. She would fill my glass without looking at me, put music on low, go and tuck up her son and come back singing, close the shutters and sing, adjust her hair and sing. I suspect she was showing off all the while, just as when she showed me stars and horses in the albums, but watching Kriska in motion I learned more.

To adjust my ear to the new language, I had to renounce all others. I followed Kriska's recommendation, except for half a dozen words in English, without which I would not have had clean clothes or a bowl of soup in my hotel room. Just in case, I resolved never to answer the phone, which, as it happens, never rang, and even abstained from radio and television, whose local programming, according to Kriska, had become infested with foreign expressions. As such, after a month in Budapest, the cadence of Hungarian words was beginning to sound almost familiar, with the stress always on the first syllable, more or less like back-to-front French. A month in Budapest actually meant a month with Kriska, because I avoided venturing into the city without her; I was afraid to lose, in the hubbub of the city, the thread of a language I was beginning to glimpse in her voice alone. I spent my days in my room, staring at the clock on the headboard and anxiously awaiting the time to head for her house, until she gave me permission to meet her as she left work. And I began to wait for her every afternoon at five at the gate of the Institute, which was not a boarding school where she taught children to read and write, as her mimicry had led me to believe, but an asylum where she told stories to the patients. She wore her backpack and, if she gave me her skates with the laces tied to hang around my neck, it was a sign that we would stroll through the streets of Pest and along the Danube on the way back to her place. The following day she would shoot off skating, and I did not mind running two miles to catch up with her at Pisti's school. But with the arrival of autumn the rains intensified and she set aside her skates. So, while one day we would sit in a café, where she would go over lessons and ask me a series of questions, the next day we would take the metro to fetch Pisti and eat at home. One day, with Kriska pressed against my chest in the packed carriage, without her asking me anything, I got it in my head to pronounce the word *szívem. Szívem* means my heart, and I looked her in the eyes as I spoke to see if my pronunciation was correct. Kriska, however, looked down, to the sides, at the window, the advertisements, the tunnel, her eyes avoiding the topic.

Pisti was the same age as my son, but small, and had his mother's wide face with prominent cheekbones, thin lips, straight but black hair and imperative tone of voice. While Kriska prepared dinner, he would drag me off to play football in a yard at the bottom of the cul-de-sac almost in the dark. He made me goal-keeper, showered me with penalties and appreciated that I flung myself on the rocky, sopping ground. After gaining his trust, my face splattered with mud, I thought he would be willing to chat. Ball round, I said, or shoe magnificent, or Kósta tired, but he did not collaborate, looking at me with a dull expression. The same look as that of the chambermaid, the concierge and the hotel staff when I began to approach them in Hungarian. Every day, however, I grew prouder of my knowledge and was little concerned that all Hungarians gave me that fish-eyed look. Like the fellow sitting beside me in the train, when, for lack of a better idea, I commented: Carriage fragrant. That Sunday I was taking the metro alone for the first time and, being anxious, I got off at Újpest-Városkapu instead of Kriska's station, Újpest-Köszpont, which was the next one. Kriska had invited me to lunch. She was making spaghetti Bolognese just for the two of us, and I decided to call her from a public phone. There was no need to call, it was pure exhibitionism, as I had just formulated a five-word sentence: There I am arriving almost. Kriska: What was that? I repeated the phrase. Kriska, cunning: I didn't hear you. Me, shouting: There I am arriving almost! Kriska, begging: Again! Me, idiot: There I am arriving almost! Kriska, who was not really the laughing sort, was in fits of laughter because of a stupid badly placed adverb: Just once more! That day I entered her house with the intention of settling accounts and wrapping up that shit of a course. But before leaving I would make a proclamation in Portuguese, in very obscene Brazilian Portuguese, with oxytone words ending in ão, names of indigenous trees and African dishes that would terrify her, a vernacular that would reduce her Hungarian to zero. I didn't do it due to Kriska's evident regret; she only didn't ask forgiveness because there is no such word in Hungarian, or rather, there is but she abstained from using it because she considered it a Gallicism. As a colloquial means of begging forgiveness, there is the Magyar expression *végtelenül büntess meg*, that is, punish me infinitely, in an imperfect translation. This was what she said to me, knowing I would understand not the words but the sincere sentiment invested in them. She stroked my face with her fingertips, closed her eyes and whispered *végtelenül büntess meg*, after which she kept her lips parted, and I understood her to be asking me to kiss her on the mouth. I kissed her, and her lips were not as solid as they looked. By the second kiss she was already kissing me more than I was her, and after her mouth she offered me her neck, recoiled with a case of the tickles, slipped from my arms, ran away. I found her in

67

the penumbra of her bedroom, waiting for me beside the bed. In a single movement she pulled her dress over her head, and seeing her completely naked made me giddy. White, white, white, I said, beautiful, beautiful, beautiful, and when my words ran out I froze. I was afraid to pull her to my chest in a frenzy and say the things I only knew how to say in my language, filling her ears with words that were indecorous, perhaps African. And she stood there before me as quiet as I was, possibly because she also feared speaking words that she still had not taught me. Finally, she pulled back the bedspread, lay down, held out her arms and said: Come. I wavered a little, as I could barely make her out in that half-light, and she said: Come. So white was her skin that it was almost impossible to make out the contours of her body against the linen sheet, and she said: Come. I lay down with Kriska, and to embrace her better I remembered Vanda.

There is no life outside Hungary, says the proverb, and as she took it literally, Kriska never concerned herself with who I had been, what I did, where I came from. A city called Rio de Janeiro, its tunnels, viaducts, cardboard shacks, the faces of its inhabitants, the language spoken there, the vultures and the hang gliders, the colours of the dresses and the sea air; for her all this was nothing, the substance of my dreams. In the middle of a lesson I might happen to think of Sugarloaf Mountain, for example, or a boy with a shaved head smoking marijuana, or Vanda arriving home from her trip, Vanda asking after me, Vanda wrapped in a white towel, but if Kriska caught me looking distracted she would clap her hands and say: Reality, Kósta, back to reality. And our reality, in addition to the daily lessons, was the Budapest of alternate weekends when Pisti stayed with his father. This ex-husband, with whom she only communicated through her son, who one would deposit at school for the other to withdraw; I could dismiss this man as a hallucination of Kriska's. Reality was outings on Margit Island with its Sunday attractions, the water acrobats on the Danube, the ram races, the Slovenian marionettes, the choir of ventriloquists. Reality was literary gatherings at the Belles-Lettres Club, the revolving disco at the top of Átila Tower, late-night visits to Obuda, the old Buda, and the thatched restaurants where we ate raw pizza. And the bottle of Tojak wine that we would take home to drink on her divan while listening to Hungarian operettas. And the heart-rending ballad of Bluebeard's daughter that she taught me, which I sang a cappella with the voice of a Hungarian baritone, bringing her to tears. And Kriska naked, holding out her arms and asking me to punish her, then Kriska unconscious, lying crosswise on the bed on the black silk sheet I had given her, twisted under her resplendent body, my toothmarks stamped on her shoulder. And Kriska's raspy breathing and me shaking her, begging her to say something, what thing? Anything. What do you mean, anything? How to count to ten. *Egy . . . kettö . . . három . . . négy . . .* in spite of all her good will she never got to five, she dozed off easily and slept deeply. Then I would get up; she had never told me whether I could sleep with her. I would pick my clothes up off the floor and avoid looking at her, because Kriska mute and inert in a foetal position was unreal, a body too perfect, its surface too smooth, the texture mysterious. I would leave after the metro had stopped running and there were no more taxis; even people in the street grew scarce with the coming of winter. I would walk for half an hour to the centre of Pest, thinking of drinking something hot, but there were no bars open. I had another half-hour of marching under a heavy sky, and sometimes I leant on the edge of the bridge to look at the Danube, black, silent. It would take me a while to convince myself that it was moving, and the odd car would always stop near by, waiting to see if I would throw myself off or not. But the true winter arrived overnight, and this night Kriska insisted on lending me a cap and overcoat smelling of mothballs. They were the vestiges of a large-headed man with a torso that was shorter than mine: the thick woollen overcoat was tight around my armpits, stopping me from lowering my arms. I would walk down the middle of the street, with a monkey-like gait, and could cross the city without meeting a soul. A moist wind blew, and even with the cap pulled down over my ears I couldn't stop to look at the river any more. I quickened my step until I got to the hotel, and not infrequently jumped over the counter to get my key, as the night doorman generally slept on the job. I would shut myself in my room and the heating burnt my throat, there was not enough mineral water in the mini fridge, room service never answered, I ran out of cigarettes. The wool blanket was itchy, I scratched and scratched, dug my fingers into my whole body, couldn't help myself, it was like having sugar under my skin. One night, I sort of accidentally called Rio: Hi, it's Vanda, I can't take your call right now, leave your message after the tone. I called again, because Vanda wouldn't leave the boy alone at night: Hi, it's Vanda, I can't take your call right now . . . I called again and again and again until I realised I was calling for the pleasure of hearing my mother tongue: Hi, it's Vanda . . . On a whim, I left a message after the tone, because it had been three months, or four or more, since I had last spoken my language: Hi, it's José. There was an echo on the line, it's José, creating the impression that my words had strayed from my mouth, Vanda, Vanda, Vanda, Vanda. And then I had a field day and said Pão de Açúcar, *marimbondo, bagunça, adstringência,* Guanabara; I said words at random, just to hear them back.

Kriska had not been too extreme when she recommended that I avoid other languages during my course of study. After a night of speaking my language and dreaming that Kriska spoke Portuguese, I found myself without the mouth for Hungarian, like a musician blowing an instrument in vain. I spent the afternoon at cross purposes with the airline employee, who made me spell out each word, her own Hungarian abstruse due to her French accent. By the time I arrived at the gate of the Institute it was dark and Kriska had already gone; I was reluctant to continue on to her house, but I went. She greeted me in great distress and said she had called the hotel, the police, the hospital and the morgue. I held her cold hands, and I think she was already beginning to imagine the things I had thought of telling her on my way there. I had tacked together a text in my head that was sincere in my feelings for her, as well as a quick explanation for my departure. I would mention, by the by, a sickly child, an elderly spouse, among other nuisances in my faraway country, and should something sound unconvincing in my speech, it would be attributed to my imprecise vocabulary and poor translation of my thoughts. At point-blank range, however, looking into Kriska's eyes, her hands slipping from mine, the only word that came to me in her language was farewell. I don't understand, said Kriska, and I repeated: *Viszontlátásra.* My mouth was dry, my articulation hesitant, and she smiled uneasily: Again! Just once more! And me: *Viszontlátásra! Viszontlátásra!* I finally made myself understood, as Kriska went quiet for a good few minutes. And suddenly she let forth a torrent of difficult words, and I'm not sure if she was expelling me from the room or asking for mercy, if she was begging me for a hot drink, accusing me of having cast a spell on her, stolen some object, a gold watch perhaps, watch? Is there watch thy evident, I retorted, bewildered, pointing at the piece of junk on her wrist, but that wasn't it, and Kriska, already upset because of the farewell, became exasperated by my ignorance. I then renounced the Magyar language once and for all, let my face, shoulder and arms fall, and she threw herself at me, clung to me and dug her fingers in as if she intended to bury then in my back, because I was a cruel man, or formidable, or dreadful, because I was spoiling the most precious moments of her life. I even thought she wanted sex, and ran my tongue behind her ear. Then she shoved me off, turned her face away and in my fleeting glimpse it seemed she had two blood clots instead of eyes. She walked slowly to the window, wedged her fingers between the wooden slats of the shutters and stood there with her back to me, trembling a little. I paced around the living room a few times, went to her bedroom, dropped her ex-husband's overcoat and cap on the bed. I went into the bathroom, the kitchen, paced around the living room a few more times and remembered that I owed her for two lessons: six thousand forints. I left the money on the table under the thermos, but it seemed odd, so I took it back. I opened the door, it was snowing out, I left anyway.

There were blizzards

THE PLANE TOOK OFF LATE, there were blizzards throughout Europe, I ended up in Copenhagen, missed my connection in Paris and was sent to Buenos Aires, but I was happy to arrive home close to midnight. The boy would be sleeping, and even Vanda would soon be going to bed. She would be sipping wine, or closing the curtains, or taking a shower, or standing in front of the mirror, plucking out grey hairs. I felt it was important to catch her off guard, wanted to see the nature of her surprise as she greeted me. I turned the key, in the living room there was a Christmas tree, Vanda was in the bedroom, I heard her voice from the corridor: Women are more adventurous in summer, they need to show their bodies . . . I must have opened the door with great force, as the nanny, who was sitting on the edge of the bed,

75

leapt up. But the boy did not move and remained leaning against the headboard with his eyes glued to the television. I didn't know Vanda now presented the evening news and at first glance it looked as though her head had shrunk. Then I realised she had lightened her hair, straightened her curls, and was wearing mascara, drop earrings, a blouse with a collar and a men's jacket with shoulder pads. No sooner had I sat down with the boy than she wrapped up the interview with the fashion designer, announced the following variety show and wished us an excellent evening. I turned to my son, but he had fallen asleep sitting up, leaning against the pillow. I put my arms round him and tried to lift him, but he was heavy; the nanny had made herself scarce and I didn't have the strength to carry him to his room. It wasn't even possible to shift his body and lay him flat; I had to go to the foot of the bed and pull him by his ankles. I took off my shoes, my woollen clothing, and in my underpants settled into an exiguous space, because in the meantime the boy had moved across the bed diagonally. I switched on the lamp; there was an interior-design magazine on Vanda's bedside table and a discussion among teenagers with pimples and piercings on their faces on TV. Under the magazine I found a piece of paper with a telephone number, unfamiliar handwriting. In Vanda's drawer, clips, pins, elastic bands, a nail file, a pen cap and a jewellery box with a baby tooth in it. The answering machine was blinking: Hi, it's José, Vanda, Vanda, Pão de Açúcar, *marimbondo, baguñçá, adstrin-gência* . . . A police patrol film was beginning, with a white officer and a black one, but I was unable to follow the plot; every time I heard car sounds I went to the window to see if it was Vanda. And there were squealing tyres, slamming breaks, spinouts, gunshots that left the boy fidgety, rubbing his eyes. One moment, when he seemed half-awake, I ran my fingers through his hair and asked: Joaquim darling, where's Mummy? He covered his face and moaned; the film was definitely interfering with his dream and couldn't have been good for his development. I managed to push him away a little with my feet, extracted a pillow from his arms, lay down and turned off the lamp and the TV. I turned it back on a short while later, because I preferred shootouts and the roar of engines to the silence of Vanda not returning. But a sex show had come on with a big-breasted presenter, and when a car horn sounded downstairs, I recognised Vanda's honking; she was always impatient with the automatic gate. I had a look and it really was a dark-coloured 4×4 going into the garage of the building. I went back to bed and tried to concentrate on the programme so as not to greet her with anxious eyes the minute she appeared in the room. A clip came on with three naked women groping one another, white, black and Oriental, then the presenter came back on holding a duck, Vanda never arrived, and I nudged the boy: Where's Mummy? The programme finished, the station went off air, all traffic stopped outside, and even so I went to the window and sat on the sill, allowing the hypothesis that Vanda might come on foot. I stared at the street, deserted except for a chap on the pavement with a cigarette in his mouth. The fellow glanced at my window from time to time and I got it into my head that he was also waiting for Vanda. I lit a cigarette as well, kind of to mark my territory, and he lit another from the butt of the first in response, perhaps to prove that he was waiting for her more than I was. But at daybreak I discovered it was the night watchman of the building, then remembered the boy's school and went to shake him by the shoulders. When he opened his eyes, I asked: Where's Mummy? Where's Mummy? He began to bawl; he was missing a few teeth, and the nanny came into the room to take him away. I sprawled across the centre of the double bed, but soon realised I really wasn't going to get any sleep. I found my dressing gown in its usual place and did the rounds of the flat; the boy was eating waffles and the nanny was laughing in the kitchen. And the maid was singing, and the cook was whistling; when the lady of the house sleeps out the help will let their hair down.

I demanded that my son be taken to school and ordered an omelette and fresh peeled fruit, but they had not been to the market and the boy was on holiday.

The lift made a grating noise, footsteps outside the door; by that time perhaps I didn't even care whether it was Vanda or not. More grating, silence, silence, silence, I opened the door: the newspaper had been left on the doormat. Moisés denies bribes in oil pipeline, read the headline, and directly underneath, in letters I could barely make out, there was something like: According to the handsome spokesman ... I went to the bedroom to fetch my reading glasses, rummaged through the pockets of the clothes I had travelled in, my holdall, and nothing. I put the maid in charge of searching through my baggage, sat in the living room and plucked a magazine from the Indian basket. It was a fashion magazine, and I leafed through it glancing at pictures and titles: Skirting Around, In Stitches, Belt Up, Eye for an Eye, Tooth for a Tooth. I tossed aside the magazine, became engrossed in the winking of the Christmas tree and smoked one, two, three cigarettes; I intended to drop in at the agency but was in no hurry. Only the cleaning lady would be there so early in the morning, the secretary at most. And under exceptional circumstances, Álvaro, if it was the day to balance the books. In this case he would be incommunicado, locked in his office with the accountant, checking the company's turnover, expenses, tax due, net income, his and my share of the profits. I imagine that when making out a nominal cheque to be credited into my bank account, even stealing a little, Álvaro would feel cheated. A bit crooked, lying on the L-shaped sofa, I poked about in the basket for another magazine and found a mustard-coloured paperback. It was peculiar to come across a book in the magazine basket; Vanda did not tolerate things out of place. Virgo rising, she would say, and normally would have already placed it on the shelf of mustard-coloured books. I held it away from my face, squinted and tried to decipher the squiggles at the top of the cover, and they were gothic letters. They were such a deep red they looked like ink blots, and the title I read was a mirage, the name of the author was a trick of my imagination. I went on to the balcony, held the cover in the sunlight, read it, reread it, and the title was the same, *The Gynographer*, by Kaspar Krabbe. It was my book. But it couldn't be my book, dumped in the Indian basket, as I never gave my clients my home address. My apocryphal books I kept under lock and key in my desk at the agency, and I had not even seen this one in print. Nevertheless, there was the German's autobiographical novel, his name on the cover, on the back cover a photograph of him in a writerly pose, hand under chin. I bent the book, with my thumb ran through it page by page like a pack of cards, and in a split second I saw thousands of illegible words pass in reverse, like an anthill in a flurry. Until I arrived at the first page, naked, with a clear dedication, the letters a little unsteady, but big: For Wanda, a memento of our tête-à-tête, enchanted, K.K. Enchanted, tête-à-tête, Wanda, I didn't understand that dedication. I looked at the book in my hands and didn't understand that book. I looked at the mustard cover, the scarlet gothic letters, I looked at the back cover and didn't understand the German's bald head, the enchanted, the tête-à-tête, I looked at the cook who appeared with a cup of coffee and didn't understand that cook, with my thumb I opened the book like a fan, and like a fan the book riffled shut, always returning to that white page, the dedication, Wanda, memento, tête-à-tête, enchanted, K.K., the big letters, I didn't understand that bell in my head, and it was the telephone ringing in the kitchen. I went to answer it, but the nanny had already handed it to the boy: Mummy . . . Mummy . . . Mummy . . . Mummy . . . he said, stuck in the groove. I took the receiver in time to hear Vanda: And who is it that sings my hat it has three corners to Joaquim? Vanda, I whispered, where are you? She was at the hotel. What hotel? I asked between clenched teeth, the three domestics watching

81

me. She had been transferred to São Paulo, why São Paulo? Because, come now, the evening news was produced in São Paulo and from Monday to Friday Vanda went on air on national television. It was an upgrade in her career, she said, to such an extent that in the area of Higienópolis everyone stopped her in the street and it could get a bit tiresome. She said that on the other hand she loved the cultural effervescence of the city and had been to scores of exhibitions. She dined at magnificent restaurants late in the evening and in the afternoons worked out at the gym. Not to mention that three times a week she went for speech therapy, because her vocal cords were showing fatigue-related problems. She was thinking about renting a flat, but at the same time she felt more protected in a hotel. She also said she had requested that management change the mattress, and her back was better as a result, then she asked what Budapest was like. I wavered, not knowing where to begin, and she took the opportunity to say she would be coming on the first flight on Saturday and asked to speak to her son again. I heard: And who's going to bring Santa Claus to Joaquim? I ran to the bedroom, because on the extension I would be free to ask her to explain the book. I picked up the phone, heard the boy saying Mummy . . . Mummy . . . Mummy . . . and there was a busy signal on the other end: Vanda had already hung up. I got the number of the hotel from the nanny, but in Vanda's room nobody answered.

K – r – a – b – b – e, I spelled, holding out the phone book to the maid, since she had given up looking for my glasses. The German answered in a sleepy voice and went quiet when he heard my name. I repeated hello, hello, it's José Costa, and he stayed quiet. I had hoped he would respond naturally: Hi, José Costa, I'm fine, and you? You disappeared, the book's great, I'll send you a copy today, you too, bye. It would be implicit that at some stage he had dedicated the book to a Vanda, without ever suspecting she was my wife. It was not unlikely that he had seen her around, as I myself had first seen her walking down the street arm in arm with her twin sister Vanessa, surrounded by a group of young people. He would easily have been enchanted by her, as I had fallen for her all of a sudden that night, although by strict choice, because I had not hesitated between her and another who was identical to her. Then he would have followed her, just as I had done an about-turn and gone into a music hall, where I stood behind her to watch a rock concert and sang all the songs without knowing any of them. One would expect him to approach her, as I had offered the twins a lift at the exit and suggested we stop at a bar in Lagoa, where we had a beer and I talked about my doctorate in language and literature, my knowledge of languages, and I even told them that turtle in German was toad plus shield and they had a fit of laughter; goodness knows if they'd been smoking something. Then Vanda began telling stories that I don't recall, but would be able to recall by lip-reading, as I still remember so well those lips that I observed as the German would have observed the colour of her shoulders, and the white sliver of her breasts in her low neckline, as he would have observed the way she walked when she went to the toilet with her sister, and as I, having eyes only for her, thought it obvious that she would return alone. I could never criticise him for having used the same arguments as mine, and pleaded the pleas that I pleaded to take her to his, as I took her to my bachelor's pad. It would make no sense to wish him ill for having done what I would have done if I were him, such as ask her to remove her underclothes before her outer garments and so on and so forth. And when dropping her off home in the small hours, if I were him, I would also have taken a copy of *The Gynographer* from the glove box, which I would have rested on her thighs in the dark of the car and dedicated to Wanda, memento of our tête-à-tête, enchanted, K.K., even knowing that she would only read the last page, in the lift. And judging it a very thin, flimsy book, unfit to occupy the bookshelf, she would fling it in the magazine basket. And there she would forget it, as she would forget the German, who would also forget her, as she had been forgetting her husband who was forgetting her in Budapest, and there you go. The only thing left to say to the German now would be: How are you? Couldn't be better, I was overseas, how's our book going? I'm dying to see it, OK, take care, bye. But no, after a long pause he said: What do you want from me? And his exacerbated accent was a sign that he had lost his composure. Feeling him cornered like that spurred me on, made me want to be rude: I need to see you now. And he said: Is this call some kind of threat? I'm waiting for you at my place, I said, and to finish off: You must know where I live. I was going to slam down the phone in his face, but he beat me to it.

I took a scalding shower, shaved at the same time, and it slowly dawned on me that the German had looked for me at the agency in order to present me with a copy of his book. Learning I was overseas, he had asked for my address and Álvaro had given it to him inadvertently, his thoughts elsewhere. Instead of sending it through the post, mistrusting as he was of our public services, he had decided to deliver it to its destination in person; he wanted to make sure the book reached the hands of the man whose generous literature had attributed to him words and thoughts of which his mind would never have conceived. He thought he'd leave the book in the care of a private secretary, or a relative, even his wife if the man were married, someone reliable who, when he returned, would simply say: A bald foreigner dropped it off and left. Before leaving he would write a note or brief dedication capable of expressing all of his gratitude without jeopardising the man's professional secrecy. It happened, however, that when he was greeted by a woman of thirty, white pleated skirt and sleeveless blouse, chestnut hair, black eyes, brown face, legs and arms, in the room awash in the light of sunset, he felt a sudden desire to avenge himself of the generous man. He introduced himself: Kaspar Krabbe, of whom you have doubtless heard, not so much as a well-published author in Germany, but more as a friend of your absent husband José. Then the woman's countenance faded, her eyes lost their sparkle, her skin became grey, a shadow covered her entirely; in the light from the balcony another woman appeared, the exact likeness of the first, like a queen from the same deck of cards, although of a higher suit. This was undoubtedly José Costa's wife, who quickly invited him to take a seat, confirming that she knew him by name, not through her circumspect husband, but through references in literary supplements. She proposed a drink, requested that the other woman fetch some ice and expressed regret that she did not have access to his literature in the original. Her tennis skirt brushed past him; she opened a cabinet in the corner of the room, pulled out a bottle of precious whisky. The essence of the style is diluted even in the best translations, she said in a singsong voice, just as the other woman arrived with the bucket of ice. And added: The only thing Vanessa and I know about German is that turtle is lizard plus shield. I can fix that, said Kaspar Krabbe, and whipped *The Gynographer*, his first creation in Portuguese, out of the envelope. I should like to present you with this book, Mrs Costa, in the manner of the citizens of Hamburg, offering a few passages for your appreciation, as one provides wine for tasting. He stood, read no more than the first two pages, and when he made mention of leaving, he heard José's wife say: Do not leave, please, we wish for more. He thus continued with his reading and took pleasure in the sound of his own voice; even his moderate accent sounded appropriate, because José Costa, with mysterious ingenuity, had succeeded in imbuing the writing with a moderate accent. Night fell, it occurred to no one to turn on the lights, and the half-light became Kaspar Krabbe; he knew that it obliterated his almost ridiculous figure, his doll-like head, and soon all that would be seen of him would be two blue eyes, suspended in the room six feet from the ground. Eyes that sparkled when he pronounced the names of the

women who throughout the story brought him pleasure and suffering, all with chestnut hair, black eyes,
all with equally brown faces, legs and arms, except
under their knickers and on their small breasts, the
colour of sand. Now unable to see the text, Kaspar
Krabbe recited it from memory with self-assurance,
and a second before complete darkness fell, he saw the
half-open lips of José's wife, a tear in the corner of her
left eye, the glass of ice in her right hand, her legs
folded on the sofa, occupying the place of the other
woman; he knew the other woman had left by her
footsteps on the carpet and the faint sound of the door
shutting. And Kaspar Krabbe continued with his recital, his licked finger turning the pages and running
down them, as if locating by touch each paragraph,
phrase and comma, and with each comma intense
breathing could be heard from José's wife; it was
evident that, although she was José's wife, this was
an abandoned woman, and seeing her in his arms at the
end of his reading, Kaspar Krabbe stepped up his pace.
Vanda was indeed about to surrender to the German,
and I would have preferred not to carry on imagining
such a scene. Yet the scene was dark, and listening to
Vanda's breathing gave me pleasure. I needed to enjoy
the sound of my words; in fact, I was anxious for the
moment when Vanda would succumb to my words.
Then Kaspar Krabbe said: And my beloved, of whose

milk I had partaken, made me drink from the water in which she had washed her blouse. And closed the book. And fell silent, aware that any further word, from his brutish mind, could freeze and harden José's wife, just as contact with his slippery skin might repel her. Possessed, Kaspar Krabbe leapt upon the woman without undressing, laid her in an L on the L-shaped sofa and took her like that. Upon completing the act he shouted Gothic words, then asked what her name was again, patted his jacket for a pen and wrote the dedication in enormous letters, as the blind write. And he wrote Vanda with a W, to attest that for one night she had been Wanda, a German's woman. Before closing the door, he thought he heard a child crying at the back of the flat. As for Vanda, she heard neither child nor door, tossed the book into the Indian basket and fell asleep. And there she left it deliberately so I would notice it, pick it up, bend it and run through it page by page like a pack of cards and read the dedication and know that for one night she had belonged to an authentic writer, if I ever decided to return from Budapest.

I used Vanda's shampoo, conditioner, a hair-volumising emulsion and dried myself with her towel. I chose a sporty outfit and tennis shoes with shock absorbers that made me almost as tall as the German. But when the porter called on the intercom to say that a gentleman was on his way up to my flat, I stopped in the middle of the living room; I truly had not believed he would have the courage to respond to my call, and I was suddenly unsure as to how to proceed. Should I demand a retraction? Slap him on the cheeks with a glove? Challenge Kaspar Krabbe to a duel? The doorbell rang, I walked on tiptoe to the door, peeped through the spy-hole, and the sight of Álvaro's bulbous nose filled me with jubilation. I opened the door and flung my arms open, but after months without seeing me he greeted me with: Look, mate, I gave him my word, I promised him you wouldn't do anything daft. He had heard of my arrival through the German, who, by the looks of things, had also told him details of his adventure with my wife. And Álvaro had the audacity to come to my place to intervene on behalf of that weasel. He told me in that weedy voice of his that a scandal would be detrimental to my own reputation, that I should think about the shame it would bring on Vanda, my son's surname; he mentioned trustworthiness. If it was about money, he said a friendly agreement would be reached, because, after all, I had signed a pro forma contract for a private service for non-commercial purposes. The German's autobiographical novel would be just another little book in my drawer, had Álvaro not become his literary agent and developed a marketing strategy to optimise the product. These were his words. Now, having done the accounts on the successive reprints of the book, and considering the prospect of overseas sales and possible screen adaptation, it was fair that I should receive something under the counter. Kaspar Krabbe was not attached to money, according to Álvaro, and even a success handed to him on a silver platter like that he had honestly been reluctant to accept. But when he finally accepted it, he became stingy about it, shuddered to think that one day he might lose it and could not even entertain the idea of sharing it with me. He went out late every night to buy the following day's papers, which he scrutinised right there at the news-stand, scanning the cultural sections for an article of mine, a letter of mine in the readers' section, a paid public notice claiming authorship of *The Gyno-grapher*. On autograph nights, during radio interviews or television talk shows, even during an informal chat with Vanda on the evening news, he was tense, glanced from side to side, twisted around, imagined that I might burst in at any moment to unmask him. He thus had reason to panic upon receiving my untimely phone call so early that morning, and Álvaro's giving his word and promising I wouldn't do anything daft had been pointless. I needed to provide Kaspar Krabbe with ample proof, said Álvaro, that I would not risk losing an honourable life, not to mention a good deal, in exchange for heights to which I had never aspired. I needed to provide evidence that I was still the old José Costa, so careful about his own name, who would not give up his anonymity for anything in the world.

On our way to the agency, with the windows closed, Álvaro's car smelled of the same cologne as it had in our student days, when he used to give me lifts home to my father's place. I lived out in the suburbs at the time, but for Álvaro the petrol was cheap, considering the essays I forged in his name, which were awarded higher marks than my own. Twenty-seven miles a day, sitting side by side, was distance enough for us to get to know one another, and admire one another out of the corner of our eyes, confide in one another, rile one another, sometimes argue at the top of our lungs. A certain instinct, however, always held us back when one came close to humiliating the other, or opening his heart too much. With a minimum of propriety and preserving a certain amount of hatred, our friendship was consolidated; contrary to love, which overflows continuously, friendship needs its dykes. As such, Álvaro never enquired as to what my father did for a living, or what had become of my mother, for example, just as I never asked him why the devil he used so much of that cologne. And now, even a little queasy, I felt comfortable in his car; complying with his request had a nostalgic flavour. It seemed to me that we were even again, because by mentioning Vanda's professional meeting with the German he had absolved her of my sordid thoughts, as if responding to a silent plea of mine. I believe, however, that he still felt he owed me something in this exchange, because he also informed me of his decision to restore the original conditions of our partnership, splitting the management and income of Cunha & Costa down the middle with me. He was polite, Álvaro was; he asked if the air-conditioning was bothering me, was happy for me to smoke in the car and put on a CD of classical music. He stood aside for me as we entered the lift, opened the door of the agency for me, and from the reception area I was pleased to see my little room intact, my dictionaries, my swivelling chair. The receptionist was not at her post, and Álvaro pointed to his office at the other end of the suite. I always felt a little uncomfortable crossing my old place of work, cluttered with furniture and lads I barely knew. But this time I saw only one desk there, with a boy of about fifteen playing pool on the computer, then I saw the windowpanes, almost opaque with a mixture of exhaust fumes and salt air, then I looked at Álvaro. He quickly said he had decided to trim company overheads for the purposes of streamlining operations, and pointed at the frames on the walls with newspaper clippings, where I made out the titles and photos of Kaspar Krabbe. On the sofa in the main office, next to the notary holding a book with a black cover, Kaspar Krabbe awaited me in flesh and blood. He rose, took two steps forward and held out his hand; he wore his customary jacket without a tie, his body still swayed slightly as if he had just stepped off a ship and he appeared to be the same man as before fame, just a mite more leisurely in each movement. The notary opened the ledger on Álvaro's desk and read out the affidavit, wherein José Costa confirmed having rendered typing services to Kaspar Krabbe, without any authorial participation in his autobiographical account *The Gynographer.* I signed the document, Álvaro signed as first witness, and the second was left to be obtained later. Then, as arranged, I retrieved from my desk the twenty cassette tapes with Kaspar Krabbe's voice recorded on both sides and handed them over to him; twenty hours of badly told, useless stories. In return, he gave gave me a copy of his, rather my, book, which he autographed there and then, in big, firm letters: To Mr José Costa, this modest writing, cordially, K.K. He apologised for his debut work which, notwithstanding its warm reception, far from satisfied his literary ambitions. Rereading it with the benefit of distance, he had found several instances of nonsense, excesses, redundancies, little imagination in the rendition of the female characters, in short, flaws he would overcome in his second volume of memoirs, already in gestation. The German spoke seriously, looking me straight in the eye, and added that he would soon be requiring my services for the dictation of his new book.

As well as displays along the entire shop window, there was a pile of them on the counter. People entered, grabbed a copy and paid at the till, when they didn't go directly to the till like someone buying a packet of cigarettes: I'll have a *Gynographer*, thanks. Others approached, had a look at the shelves, checked the prices of the imports, circled the table of recent releases, and finally ran across the pile on the counter. It's selling like hot cakes, said the shop owner, or, it'll hit a hundred thousand by Christmas, and this kind of recommendation was a dead cert; yet another gift-wrapped *Gynographer*. Planted in the centre of the tiny bookshop, in the space of a few hours, I lost count of the number of customers that left with my book. They passed me without looking at me, bumped into me without imagining who I was, and it filled me with a vanity I had not felt for a long time. Perhaps feeling I was disturbing the circulation, the shop owner eventually decided to address me: Would you like something? I said nothing, just showed him my *Gynographer* open on the title page, with the autograph, so he would see I was not a book thief. And there I stood, puffing smoke, glaring at the idiot, chewing over words of contempt, because if it weren't for my book, that dump would already have closed down. I only moved away when I saw Vanda through the display window, passing by in a sarong and straw hat, heading for the beach. Of course it wasn't Vanda; I went to look at her face and it was nothing like her, but they could have been cousins, so alike was their walk. Because no two women in the world walk identically; not models, geishas or even twin sisters. If Kriska, for instance, were to appear walking down the promenade, I would be able to pick her out a mile away. But Kriska, being Hungarian, doesn't count, and there is not a woman on the entire Rio seafront who walks like a Hungarian. On Ipanema Beach the mere thought of Kriska seemed out of place, yet I still thought about her a little. And I laughed to remember that, before getting to know her body, I had even begun to suspect there was something wrong with it, so different were her movements from Vanda's. Except when she was on skates, because on wheels the sway of the body is almost neutral and all women are alike. Sometimes, watching her walking around the living room, giving me an exercise in dictation or the like, I suggested she put them on; it was a way for me to appreciate her better, or to remember Vanda, although Vanda had never skated. Kriska complied with my requests, somewhat confused, probably thinking it was a fetish of mine. And she took to going about the house on skates, even with her son present; I actually had to ask her to stop doing it. And over time I became enamoured with Kriska's natural movements, but not to the point of forgetting Vanda; so much so that, at the end of the beach, I recognised her again in another woman, not by her gait, but precisely by the way she stayed still, sitting on a bench facing the sea. I knew very well that Vanda was in São Paulo, but I still thought, it's Vanessa, who also had that way of folding her legs to one side, as if saving a place for someone else, perhaps a habit of twins. Of course it wasn't Vanessa; she was little more than a girl, and only when I stopped behind her did I detect a sign of life, a gentle, even lifting of her shoulders, her slow breathing. I was already convinced that she was a yogi, when the abrupt gesture of her left hand startled me. I looked over her head, and she had just turned the page of a book. Only then did I realise that she was reading, and the thing in her lap looked like my book. I sat on the end of the bench next to her feet and saw that it was indeed the mustard cover of *The Gynographer*, which she read with zigzagging eyes. I also opened my copy and out of the corner of my eye followed her reading, her half-open lips, braces on her teeth. She turned the pages voraciously so as not to lose track of the adventure, or the cadence of my sentences, and was already halfway through the book when her eyes stopped at the top of an odd-numbered page; she wrinkled her forehead, appeared puzzled by a word, and I feared she would give up reading. She did in fact close the book, marking her place with an ice-lolly stick, put it away in a canvas bag, gave me a light kick as she unfolded her legs, apologised, she hadn't seen me. I pointed at the mustard cover in my hands, the coincidence, then found the title page with the dedication, said the author was my friend, but she had already gone. I looked around, the beach was emptying, people were drinking beer at the kiosks, the sun was setting behind Dois Irmãos Hill.

There was a time when, if I had had to opt between two types of blindness, I would have chosen to be blind to the splendour of the sea, the mountains, the sunset in Rio de Janeiro, so as to have eyes to read beautiful things in black letters on a white background. I went to the cinema, extraordinary women paraded across the screen, the films were in a language I knew, and I was unable to wrest my eyes from the subtitles. But now, even if I were to find my reading glasses, I would not be inspired to open my own book, whose content I barely remembered. Nor would I touch the newspaper lying at the foot of the bed, or the volumes piled up on my bedside table, even if I were sane and alert, rather than insomniac ever since Budapest. If I already had eyestrain before thirty, it was not surprising that I had arrived at forty with a mind saturated with written words. Perhaps all I had left for them was a good ear, and in search of the most sonorous words I ran through the television channels well into the night. Maybe I would come across a programme on literary topics, with any luck a round table on my book, a pretty actress declaiming my turns of phrase. But after listening to fragments of soap operas, comedy shows, musicals, frivolities, I settled on a gangster film while waiting for Vanda's news. Already overcome by sleepiness, I saw figures on the screen and my thoughts escaped them, a little like the way the dubbed words did not fit in the actors' mouths. And when I heard Vanda introducing the news, I think I had already dozed off; I strained to open my eyes. And when I did open my eyes, I had gone blind. I rubbed them, opened them wide, but I was completely blind. I tried to stay calm, bit the pillow, concentrated on Vanda's voice, focused on her words, ministry, cold front, oil pipeline, catastrophe, tie-break . . . Her voice was very serene and melodious, and little by little it lulled me back to sleep, resigning myself to my new condition; tomorrow I would think about what to do, buy a dog, that kind of thing. At any rate, tomorrow Vanda would provide me with assistance, for as soon as she found out about the accident, she would most certainly take leave of absence from the news. All things considered, being blind beside Vanda for the rest of my life no longer seemed so terrible. I would go with her to the beach, the hospital, the library, restaurants, London; I would willingly follow her voice anywhere. Unencumbered by sight, I would perceive with greater discernment whether she was cheerful, whether she was lying, whether she felt sorry for me, whether she was whispering on the phone, whether she was ashamed of having a blind husband. And each night she would read me a new book, and cover my eyelids with compresses, which would only serve to endear her to me further. At times the compresses would be scalding hot, or soaked in lemon; at times Vanda would decide to remain in silence for several days, to see me fumbling around; at times she would read only the even-numbered pages of the book, but I would never complain about a thing, not even of her ageing, acquiring the equivalent of wrinkles in her voice. I would pretend not to notice that she occasionally went about crying, now for having grown old, then for having wasted her life to guide a parasite. In revenge, she would even be capable of turning up one morning propped against me, but completely cold, frozen in bed like an ice statue, and our son would let out a howl in the bedroom doorway. The boy howled like a lunatic in the corridor and, in addition to the blaring television, the light seeping through the cracks in the blinds was in my face. When I saw 9 a.m. on the alarm clock, I jumped out of bed, having resolved to give Vanda a surprise. I would arrive in São Paulo at lunchtime, pick her up at the hotel, go with her to exhibitions, the gym, the television studio and take her to dine in an Indian restaurant. But when I looked at myself in the mirror, I found a deformed face, covered in lumps, my eyes swollen; it was possible they wouldn't even let me on board looking like that. I had shaved the night before, yet my thick beard looked three days old, and then I understood that I had slept for at least thirty hours straight. I remembered the boy's howling and went to the living room; the door was open and the janitor and a taxi driver came in with piles of packages, which they deposited at the foot of the Christmas tree. I heard laughter and saw Vanda lying on top of the boy on the L-shaped sofa, rubbing her nose in his face. Her hair was wet, once again dark and curly; I had never desired any woman as I desired this one, and when she turned my way, it took her a few seconds to recognise me.

I didn't even shave, because Vanda practically booted me out of the flat. Knowing my unsociable temperament, at times aggressive, and how reporters and photographers are unscrupulous about invading domestic environments, she barely let me put on a pair of Bermuda shorts and flip-flops. She made me leave through the service door, while the crew coming to interview her came up in the front lift. I lit a cigarette in front of the building and started walking. I would have ended up on the beach if I had gone straight ahead, but I turned right, right, right and right, because I was not guided by linear thinking. My thoughts revolved around Vanda, and I went around the block many times until I saw the news van pull away from the pavement outside the building. A 4 × 4 left the garage at the same time, honked in my ear, and it was her. In the back seat was the nanny with the boy, in a national team strip that was bursting at the seams. I went upstairs alone, as the thought of going to lunch at Vanessa's place was unappealing, even if I were invited. I much preferred to make a sandwich and wait for Vanda on the balcony, smoking. I smoked until I emptied my last packet of Fecske cigarettes, crumpled it, and without Hungarian cigarettes I would give up smoking without any problems. I had already done it two years earlier, when Vanda had convinced me that Joaquim had become a passive smoker, and not even on the balcony would she let me have a puff. I crushed the Fecske packet, then regretted it; after all, from Budapest, I had only brought back one packet of cigarettes in my luggage and that written word, *fecske*. The tobacco was gone, but the Hungarian word . . . perhaps I would not be able to give it up just like that. I rested the packet on my thigh, smoothed it out, thought of tucking it away inside a book of poems to which Vanda would not have access, on a high shelf and in French. In this way, I would come to peek at it in the small hours of each night in the beginning, then every other day, then sporadically, on special dates, until one day the word *fecske*, on yellow paper with the picture of a swallow, would no longer mean a thing to me. But when I heard Vanda's voice I crushed the packet again and in a reflex action threw it down below, into the dark. And I went to assist mother and nanny, who were dragging the sleeping boy by his arms; I lifted his feet and we transported him in a horizontal position to his bed. Vanda took off his football boots and whispered for me to get his presents from the tree. I grabbed about seven packages and distributed them around the bed, where Vanda had lain down with the boy and was singing silent night, silent night, although there were still three nights to go before Christmas. I went to get a second batch and when I returned Vanda had stopped singing and was just stroking his head. When I arrived carrying a video game and a tricycle, I saw Vanda with her eyes closed, curled around her son. I retired to our bedroom and lay down, hoping that at any moment she would wake up in an uncomfortable position and come to me. She came in on tiptoe at dawn, and I let her think I was asleep. It gave me great pleasure to see the naturalness with which she removed her blouse, with no bra underneath, then unbuttoned her skirt, leaving on only her knickers, and I noticed that her time away from the sea had not changed her skin tone. When I thought she was looking for pyjamas or a nightdress, she took a light spaghetti-strap dress from a hanger and stepped into it. I got up, coughed, startling her, and before I could ask a thing, she quickly said she needed to catch the first plane to São Paulo. She turned towards the wall, said she had a brunch at the city hall, then said she had to cover an event at the racecourse, then said she had to move out of the hotel, and I couldn't work out why she was saying these things with her back to me. But she wanted help with her dress, and as I did it up I saw her skin form a slight fold, which the zip did not nip by a hair. She kissed me on the face and took off, I caught her by the arm outside the lift, and there she remembered that she had bought me a present as well. She pulled a small package from her purse and from the shape I could tell it was a book. I didn't even need to guess what book it was, because the package was mangled and I could see a little of the mustard cover and gothic letters. She apologised for having opened it on the plane; she had already read it twice and was unable to resist a third reading: It's absolutely amazing. She stepped into the lift and with the door closed repeated: Absolutely amazing.

Spoken references to my work, praising or otherwise, I had learned to listen to impassively, since the days in which I mingled with the crowd to follow recently written political speeches. When I began to write for the press, I took pleasure in visiting those bars in Copacabana where solitary men spent the afternoon drinking beer and reading newspapers. If I found someone absorbed in one of my articles, I would sit at the next table, and more often than not the fellow would soon comment on the text, never suspecting I was the author. It's just that people always strike up conversations with me, thinking they know my everyday face, as impersonal as the name José Costa, from somewhere; in a telephone book with photos, there would be more faces exactly like mine than listings for Costa José. Often the fellow would already have knocked back a few beers and would nudge me, reciting passages from the article with enthusiasm, or occasionally aversion, scorn. In the first case I allowed myself to make some kind of rebuttal, so as to inflame him even more, causing him to stand in the centre of the bar and reread the most brilliant sentences at the top of his voice; in the second I always concurred readily in order to wrap up the subject. But after I was married, on the days when I was sure I had written a text with great inspiration, I renounced the opinions of the bars; my wish was for Vanda to read it. I would buy several copies of the paper and leave them open at my article in her path, on the dinner table, on top of the telephone, in the boy's cot, next to the bathroom mirror. Seeing Vanda running her eyes across my letters, smiling faintly, appreciating one of my texts without knowing it was mine, would almost be like watching her undress without knowing I was looking. But no, she would pick up the paper and flick through the pages, looking at photographs and reading the captions; Vanda didn't have much patience for reading. Hence my stupefaction upon hearing from her own mouth that she had read my book, not once, but three times. And it was just as well that she had been in such a hurry and hadn't even looked at me when she said what she said, because at that instant I behaved like an amateur. I must have gone red, I bit my lower lip, my eyes filled with water, I felt sorry for and proud of myself; it was as if two words from her had repaired seven years of disregard. After a moment of paralysis, I realised I hadn't even thanked her for the gift. I tore down the stairs and ran to the pavement just in time to see her take off in a private taxi. I went to the chemist's, bought a pair of glasses, leant against the counter, opened the book, but I soon realised that the reading would not be enjoyable; I would have liked to have read it with her eyes. I wrapped it up again anyway to conserve it as I had received it from her, absolutely amazing. With her words ringing in my head, my own judgement of the book would be of little worth; it would be worth as much as that of the drunks of Copacabana, or that of the reviews Álvaro had sent me in a portfolio I hadn't opened. The portfolio was supposed to serve as encouragement for me to return to work: Look, mate, I can't get the German off my back, you've gotta get the new book happening, I've even swung a sponsor . . . A meeting was arranged at the agency for Kaspar Krabbe to record his story, but I didn't go, pleading fatigue; it struck me as somewhat offensive that they should expect me to mass produce bestsellers. Álvaro insisted, called me constantly, his voice reverberating in the empty agency, and had I been the spiteful sort I would have suggested that he outsource my duties. I knew his lads had abandoned him one by one, stealing his clients, setting up prosperous agencies in which anything and everything was written, except autobiographical novels of the calibre of mine. And if they did write them, they would not only charge a fortune, but they would demand to have their names at the top of the cover; after all, they belonged to this new class of renowned ghostwriters, who even appeared in magazines, arm in arm with tall women. But I didn't mention the lads to Álvaro, just asked him not to call my place so much. I might need the phone in an emergency, because those days I was alone with the boy and the nanny, besides which Vanda might want to get in touch, find out how the family was, pass on her new address in São Paulo or the number of her mobile. And when she called, I would take the opportunity to tell her how much I had appreciated her present, confessing my surprise at her literary discernment. Then, feeling proud, she would go on about the fluency of the narrative and the stylistic qualities of the book, and, having it at hand, she would read me whole passages that she had underlined. The call never came, but the waiting had the effect of bringing us closer together, my son and me; I put together his Christmas presents, a police helicopter, a fire engine, got a remote-controlled alligator up and running. We ate together in the kitchen and for Christmas Eve I got the delicatessen to deliver four panettoni. I invited him to watch the evening news in my bed and was even managing to exchange a few words with him: Who's the pretty lady on TV? Mummy. Who's the apple of Joaquim's eye? Mummy. Who's coming to spend New

Year's Eve with Daddy? Mummy. So sleep: My hat it has three corners, three corners has my hat, and had it not three corners, it would not be my hat.

I was sure I would see in the New Year with Vanda, after all, there was no evening news to keep her in São Paulo that night. We could watch the fireworks in Copacabana and, just like in the early days, we would cast white flowers into the sea, make wishes and kiss on the lips at midnight. New year, new life; in her ear I would promise never to lose sight of her again, as I was prepared to do anything to prove my love to her, including going to live in São Paulo. I really was considering giving up the agency, the books and my professional activities for good. Perhaps, as happens with many a miserable artist, my creative vein had been slashed in the prime of life. But this caused me no anguish; it would not be a reason to surrender to drink, to religions. Nor would I need to live as a recluse or in disguise, because being anonymous, and not an artist stripped of glory, I would be safe from public ridicule. I would not wallow in reminiscence, much less become a swindler, a rogue writer, forger of my own writing. And I wouldn't even experience hardship, as I already had reasonable reserves, not to mention that Vanda must have been doing well from the television. And as of zero hour she would be surprised to rediscover in me that passionate young man, his heart always on his sleeve, ready to externalise his finest sentiments. Because right at the beginning of our marriage, when I was still a modest writer, I was undoubtedly, for her, an amazing husband. But as I perfected my literature, I naturally began to relax in my treatment of Vanda. So much devotion to my craft, writing and rewriting, correcting and polishing texts, pampering every word I put on paper, left me with no good words for her. I no longer felt like manifesting myself in her presence, and when I did, it was to utter absurdities, platitudes, wishy-washy sentences with syntactical errors, unfortunate word combinations. And if at night, in bed with Vanda, enchanting words popped into my mouth, I contained them, hoarded them for future practical use. Anyway, I was sure I would see in the New Year with her, but had already acknowledged that she had reasons not to appear. I had almost accepted the idea that she was with another man, perhaps a modest man of letters from São Paulo who paid her the attention she deserved. The boy also waited for her for hours with one eye on the television, and just couldn't understand that there would be no news that night. We watched pyrotechnical spectacles in Moscow, Athens, Berlin; it all looked the same to me, and I think it was during the Lisbon New Year that I dozed off. A symphony with an orchestra and choir was playing, then faded, faded, giving way to my hat it has three corners in two voices, and it wasn't a dream that Vanda and Vanessa were singing the boy to sleep, both with sleek, blow-dried locks, earrings, diamond necklaces, bracelets, long sequined gowns. I leapt out of bed, Vanessa laughed at my boxer shorts and Vanda was surprised that I wanted to go to the party.

So hot my Lord, o-o-o, o-o-o . . . the carnival music could be heard from the lift. The door opened at the last floor and I ran across a photographer, his camera pointed at my face. I even saw my face in the lens, bug-eyed, open-mouthed, the appearance I have in all my photos, passport photos. I saw the photographer's index finger about to press the button then retreat. I swerved, and then he photographed Vanda and Vanessa, smiling, one foot in the ballroom and the other in the lift. They both remained like that for a few seconds, as if surprised in movement, before the equally frozen photographer. Until Vanessa's smile faded, she lowered her face, left the frame, and he photographed Vanda, one, two, three, four exposures. I looked around at the people all in light-coloured attire, more glittery than light, and felt that my grey suit at that party would be almost gaudy. The carnival song saturated the amplifiers: Across the Sahara desert we traipsed . . . and some people jumped up and down on the spot. The immense crowded ballroom ended in floor-to-ceiling windows overlooking Copacabana Beach; lights flashed here and there, and at times it was difficult to distinguish between the fireworks on the beach and the flashes inside. I took Vanda's hand, sought out a quieter corner for us, but in fact it was she who led me, and she sought lights, she carrying my dark body. Eventually I saw her hand let go of mine, like that of a drowned man; I saw Vanda fly almost, hurtling towards the brightest source of light in the ballroom. It was a battery of reflectors, where shining above all heads was Kaspar Krabbe's ruddy bald crown. He was giving an interview to a reporter I recognised from the TV, both in white dinner jackets, both bellowing into the microphone, but from where I was only the carnival song could be heard: From Egypt we did come . . . Before long Álvaro emerged in a golden-yellow dinner jacket, holding up a copy of *The Gynographer* for the camera, and the three of them hugged one another in fits of laughter: Allah, Allah, Allah, my good Allah . . . they appeared to be singing in chorus. That was when the reporter called Vanda over, who came on scene ebullient as I had never seen her. She stretched up on tippy-toes to exchange two kisses with Kaspar Krabbe, and I read her lips: Absolutely amazing. She shook her head and repeated: Absolutely amazing. Our faces were burnt by the sun that blazed . . . went the carnival song, and when the reflectors were turned off, I couldn't find Vanda. I wandered through the ballroom, wandered, and Vanessa appeared in my path, handed me a flute of champagne, raised hers and pulled me up the stairs to an open terrace. Across the Sahara desert we traipsed . . . it was a crooner in front of a brass band, all dressed as Hawaiians, on a stage behind the pool. Vanessa leant against the balustrade, pointed at the beach, and I think she asked me to take her to the beach, but I couldn't understand her. Our glasses were empty, I went to find a waiter and ran into Álvaro coming up the stairs with a strong-featured woman, who looked like a transvestite. Where's the German? I asked, but he consulted his watch and said eleven-thirty, then clasped my shoulders and shouted something in my ear about marketing strategy, copyright. Allah-la-o, o-o-o, o-o-o . . . now everyone was singing and jumping by the edge of the pool, their arms raised. And at the other end of the pool I caught sight of Vanda, posing again for photographers. She was sitting side-on, her legs folded over the edge, covered by her silver dress, perhaps posing as a mermaid. I would take her a flute of champagne, if I could find the waiter, but then I saw Kaspar Krabbe approaching her, two flutes in hand. She lifted her hand, causing her bracelet to slide from wrist to elbow, and even at that distance I made out the slow movement of her lips: Absolutely

113

amazing. To get around the pool I traipsed through
groups of drunks, ether sniffers, politicians, Americans, gays: Allah, Allah, Allah, my good Allah ... I
finally came to a halt in front of Vanda and Kaspar
Krabbe, sitting side by side, face to face. I stood there,
my legs quaking, watching the German talk quietly to
Vanda, and judging from his creased forehead, I
imagined he was describing his painful creation pro-
cess. I tolerated the sparkle in Vanda's eyes for some
time without realising that my hand was tensing, and
the empty flute I was clenching suddenly shattered.
The shards fell at the feet of the German, who still did
not stop speaking, and appeared to be going on and on
about the same subject, always wearing that contrite
expression. And I was already more or less decipher-
ing the words in his mouth: Many a white night was
spent, gazing long at a sheet of paper, or: Many sheets
were torn in the night, longing for words on paper, or:
Many were my long hairs that fell, on white sheets like
lines on paper, and Vanda replied: Absolutely amazing. Eventually I nudged his back, and the blood on
my fingers left a print on his white jacket. Only then
did he look at me, without much interest, and, granted,
it was not befitting that he treat me with familiarity in
public; to all intents and purposes, I was no more than
a typist who had rendered him services. Vanda, however, was my wife and looked at me with the same

114

distaste. I know my grey suit embarrassed her, she being accompanied by a formally dressed gentleman. But even if I had been half-naked in a pair of boxer shorts, I was her husband, therefore, I held out my hand and said: Come. I waggled my hand to hurry her up and said: Let's dance. She left my hand in the air, was disgusted by my hand dripping blood, and that was just not on; I had never been disgusted by her blood. I grabbed her wrist, jerked her to her feet, and she shot a glance at Kaspar Krabbe, who did not flinch. I crossed the terrace with Vanda in tow, stumbling along because of her high heels. Allah-la-o, o-o-o, o-o-o . . . I traipsed through groups of gays, Americans, politicians, and the photographer jumped in front of me and took one, two, three, four photos. Vanda covered her face, cried; I kicked the photographer, passed Álvaro, the transvestite, passed in front of the band: So hot my Lord, o-o-o, o-o-o . . . Behind the stage was a dark narrow corridor, full of black cases, like sarcophagi in the shape of musical instruments, and it was a calm corner, ideal for the two of us. Vanda resisted, dug in her heels, squatted, and I dragged her squatting into that pit, where her eyes no longer shone, nor did her dress, nor anything. There she had a tantrum, no doubt thinking I would rip off her clothes, that I would beat her and take advantage of her. I limited myself, however, to setting Vanda on

115

her feet, immobilising her with my body, and pressing her hips against the stage scaffolding, because I only intended to be alone with her for a minute. I didn't even want to shout at her, and was only waiting for the din to finish to say a few words. I held her hair with both hands, pressed my nose against hers, smelled her champagne breath, or maybe it was mine, felt our hearts beating, and that is how we remained. Until the whole band stopped on a short chord, and before the applause, rockets and racket erupted there was a split second of silence. In that hollow instant, in a voice that wasn't mine, I informed her: I am the author of the book.

The last time I faced Vanda, her eyes were wide open and her face was lit by the fireworks: gold, silver, blue, green and pink. Then I escaped down the stairs, took the vibrating lift, and the building felt like it was coming down with the fireworks. I crossed the avenue, went down to the beach crowded with people, except for a few clearings with sand sculptures of Yemanjá surrounded by candles. I reached the water's edge, where people with hitched-up skirts and rolled-up trousers were throwing white flowers into the sea. A stronger wave broke and I moved back so as not to get my shoes wet. The foam reached my feet and a bunch of lilies washed up on the sand. It meant a wish that had been refused, for being overly ambitious, or not intense enough, or enigmatic, or indecorous, who knows. I picked up the bunch with its three dripping wet flowers, withered but still intact, and thought of wading into the sea, suit and all, to throw it behind the breaking waves. But perhaps Yemanja would be displeased to see those lilies again, lilies she had just spurned. Lilies, nevertheless, are lilies, they are all alike, and surely she was not there judging lilies, but wishes. So I closed my eyes and even took two, three steps forward, until I realised I had no wish to make. I who, without believing in Yemanja, had always thrown her offerings and been granted my wishes, was now a credulous man with a useless offering in his hand. I could only have wished not to have said what I had said to Vanda. I could only have wished to erase those words, exchange them for any others, cut them out of my history, but a wish like that not even the goddess of the sea can grant. So I dropped the lilies and walked slowly through the soft sand to Copacabana Fort, then along Ipanema Beach, and I saw the sun rise from the lookout in Leblon. I let myself quietly into the flat, the bedroom door was open, Vanda was still in her silver dress. She slept all curled up, hugging herself, and I turned my eyes away, afraid to feel desire. I pulled my suitcase down from the top of the wardrobe, threw a few clothes in it and closed it quickly. From the false bottom of a drawer I retrieved my passport, credit card, some money, dollars, forints. I must have made a noise as I moved my suitcase, because Vanda said: José. I was already in the middle of the living room when I heard: I'll heat up your soup.

You big

YOU BIG SHIT EATER. Kriska slapped the table; she did not allow her son to say shit during dinner. You big dick sucker. I swallowed down my chicken, cabbage, water and bread in silence, and nonetheless, for me, the nights Pisti stayed over were cheerful. The other nights I came home from work, listened to recordings, took notes, heated up something or other in the microwave, did the dishes, set up my camp bed in the pantry, closed my eyes and invented countries. I invented historical cities, volcanoes, named the great rivers and tributaries, and if I was lucky, I would fall asleep. But I almost always awoke to Kriska's voice, off pitch. She would arrive home in the small hours because she had taken to drinking vermouth, and when she drank lots of vermouth she brought men home. And when she brought men home, she made a

119

point of taking them to see me lying there: There's
the individual I was telling you about, and the man:
That's where the sorry creature resides, and Kriska:
That's where the individual resides. Then they would
head for the bedroom and were not even considerate
enough to close the door. I would sit on my camp bed,
put my earphones on and turn the reel-to-reel recorder to full volume so I would not have to listen to
anything else. I listened to sonnets, dramas, solilo-
quies, but under such circumstances I preferred heated
debates, even if I missed half of the words, with
everyone speaking at once. I was tormented by gaps
in the recordings, poets' pauses and the faltering
voices of older speakers. Or when it was time to
change the reel and I was forced to make miscella-
neous noises, I would go nham, nham, nham, nhom,
nhom, nhom, and even then I sometimes heard moans
in the bedroom. And if I got carried away with my own
noises, they would fall about laughing in the bedroom.
To this day Kriska thinks that nham, nham, nhom,
nhom is the language spoken in South America.

When Kriska got me the job, she said: It's manual
labour, for immigrants like you. Her words were
insulting, but the job wasn't, on the contrary; were
it not for Kriska's connections at the Belles-Lettres
Club, it is doubtful they would have accepted a
foreigner, limping in the language, in their midst.

Mind you, those intellectuals, caught up as they were in semantics, semiotics and hermeneutics, never addressed subordinates. And to push furniture around, install microphones and adjust the sound, I got by with a spattering of Hungarian: excuse me, testing, one, two, three ... I took the recorder home after each session under the pretext of keeping up its maintenance, and listened to recordings incessantly to refine my language skills. The following morning I would lug the recorder back, leave the recordings in the office, collect a new supply of blank tapes and resume my post in a corner of the library. As soon as the first club member entered, I would start recording, with a standby ready, because no word uttered on the premises could be lost. Sometimes entire tapes remained blank, as the belletrists were immersed in reading, meditating, taking notes or napping in their armchairs. But before nightfall, someone would almost always pose a contemporary issue of cultural relevance for the appreciation of his colleagues. They also discussed literary classics, when a poet wasn't reciting new verses, gripped by sudden inspiration. And on Saturday nights the Belles-Lettres Club auditorium was open to the public for the literati to exhibit their work, although literature, in my mind, is the only art that does not require exhibition. I arrived three hours ahead of time, checked wires, cables and plugs, lined

121

up tables, covered them with black cloth and placed chairs behind them with a microphone facing each chair. Minutes before the curtains opened, I placed glasses and bottles of mineral water on the tables and sat at the sound desk in the wings. From there, craning my neck, I could see part of the audience without being seen; I could see if Kriska was accompanied or not, as she always sat in the first row. And although I remained in the dark, on such occasions I wore a tie and navy-blue suit I had picked up in good condition at the Bulgarian market. At the same market, with an advance on my first pay, I had bought a tight-fitting beret and an enormous bearskin coat that I didn't take off even to sleep, because pantries are not heated, and that was a hard winter even for Europeans, let alone me, who had arrived unprepared. I had not brought enough warm clothing in my hastily packed suitcase, nor had I concerned myself with this upon my arrival, assuming I would be able to use the overcoat and wool cap in Kriska's cupboard. While I did not believe that she would greet me with kisses after my abrupt departure, I never imagined that she would refuse a freezing man warm clothes that did not even have her smell on them. The overcoat and cap of an ex-husband; I could argue that in some ways they were more mine than hers. But Kriska was not open to discussion. I think she only took me in because she did not want any problems with the police in the event of my dying at her gate.

I had telephoned Kriska as soon as I had checked into the Plaza Hotel. I left my whereabouts on her answering machine, in my best pronunciation, and waited in vain for her to return the call. On the second day I sent her flowers and a note: Dear Kriska, in Budapest eternally I am, Kósta. Nothing. On the third day I decided to meet her at the front gate of the asylum. I saw a silhouette that looked like hers in a window, but if she left it was through a back exit. Night fell, I took the metro, went to 84 Tóth Street and rang house number 17 on the intercom. I rang and rang but no one answered; it grew colder, the metro was closed and I returned to the hotel at a brisk march. The following afternoon I identified myself at the asylum and asked after Kriska, but the woman I spoke to just stared at me; she must have been a patient. I went to the back exit, circled the asylum seven times, poked my head in the cafés we used to haunt together, and had just about convinced myself that Kriska was holidaying at a ski or ice-skating resort. I headed to her house through force of habit, rang the intercom without much hope, and when I heard Pisti's hello, I rejoiced: Here friend Kósta! Here goalie Kósta! Pisti said nothing, did not open the electric gate and left me standing a good while in the damp night air. My fingers were already numb and my ear felt like a glass shell when he returned to the intercom, put on a deep voice and stated that Ms Fülemüle no longer lived there. On the fifth day my lungs were rasping; I'm not sure if it was because of the Fecske cigarettes or the beginnings of pneumonia. I decided to buy gloves, a beret and a cashmere coat in a large department store, but when I went to pay, the women refused my credit card. What your reason is? I enquired, but the woman was peeved, I think she spoke in a dialect, and did not even want to see my passport. I stopped at a cash machine, typed in my pin number, an incomprehensible message appeared and the money did not come out. I repeated the operation, the screen went dark and the machine swallowed my card. My first thought was, it's Álvaro; he's frozen my bank account as a form of blackmail to get me slaving away in the back room of the agency again. Then it dawned on me: it's Vanda who wants me back, to take me to parties, to introduce me to hoards of friends, to whom she has confided: My husband is the true author of *The Gynographer*. I stood there for a moment glaring at the screen, but insulting the machine would have been as inappropriate as kicking Vanda for what I myself had told her. I lost myself in the busiest streets of Pest, went into and out of shopping centres, got on and off trains and sought bars full of people speaking Hungarian; I thought that in this manner I might forget the words I had spoken to Vanda. I managed, sort of, knowing all the while that they were lurking nearby, like background music, a constant drone behind my thoughts. Perhaps, in order to forget those words, I needed to forget the actual language in which they had been spoken, just as we move from a house that reminds us of the dead. Perhaps it was possible to replace one language with another in my head, little by little, discarding a word for every word acquired. For a time, my head would be like a house undergoing renovations, with new words being hoisted up through one ear and the rubble being lowered down through the other. I would of course be saddened to see so many beautiful words, wainscoting, going to waste all because of a few disastrously employed pieces. On the other hand, however, once free of my entire Latin vocabulary, with Kriska's help I would learn to speak Magyar flawlessly. And if Kriska insisted on not receiving me, then I would learn the Hungarian of the streets, of the whores, of the ale houses, of a sleazy dive where I drank that afternoon and on into the night until they closed the doors. Back on the street a fine drizzle was falling, which made me walk fast, run, gallop towards Buda. I was already in the middle of the bridge when I realised I couldn't go back to the hotel. By that time, my name on a confiscated credit card would surely be on some blacklist, and at any moment the manager of the Plaza would demand that I pay my expenses. I had spent my last forints on beer and cigarettes and would thus be detained and repatriated, without appeal. I did an about-turn, ran two miles, walked a few more and dragged myself to Kriska's gate. I rang the intercom and prayed that she would answer; it was raining heavily and I was drenched. When I tried to ring again, I was unable to raise my hand, which, rigid and ashen, fingers stuck together, looked more like the paw of a strange animal, twisted inward. It occurred to me to seek shelter of any kind, a garage, a graveyard tomb, but my knees balked; I was frozen to the spot. I was unwittingly becoming hunchbacked, and burying my neck between my shoulders afforded me some comfort. I screwed up my face, closed my eyes and stuck my chin on my chest; while I still had air in my lungs, I could breathe on my chest, heat it a little with my own vapour. The chill in my lower limbs also began to lift because I could no longer feel my legs, which suddenly folded, I don't know how. I fell to my knees and my forehead hit the iron bars of the gate, but the impact did not hurt; I only heard the sound reverberating in my head. Afterwards, I felt warm blood running down my face and thought I could probably sleep a little in that position. That's how I was when I heard a car engine behind me, doors closing, laughter, footsteps, then a man's voice: So what's this then? And a woman's voice: That's the individual I was telling you about, and the man: The sorry creature is on the verge of death, and the woman: On the verge of death the individual at my gate is.

I awoke in pyjamas on a divan, under covers, my head in bandages. I looked at Kriska and was a little afraid of her thin lips. I began to babble about my destitution, my homelessness in Budapest, said I had escaped political persecution in my own country and many times I heard her sigh. But it was my Hungarian, so prematurely deteriorated, that was the cause of her grief. And she made me stop, justifiably hurt, because the language unlearned like that, for her, must have been like her white skin, which I had so quickly forgotten. She ordered me to my feet and I began to shake all over with foreboding, certain I was about to be kicked back out on the street, fever and all. But Kriska was kind: she put me up in her pantry, where there was a canvas camp bed and a short blanket like the ones on planes. I don't know how many days I spent convalescing there, because it was an enclosed environment with a two-hundred-watt bulb that was always on. I only got up to go to the bathroom, and the mirror gave me a vague idea of the passing of time as I saw my beard growing and the gauze rotting around my head. After bathing I would put my dirty pyjamas back on and, disgusted with myself, go back to bed. I would occasionally catch sight of Kriska, when she changed my plate and left me a glass of water and saucer with my antibiotics. She barely spoke to me, perhaps through modesty, just as she would not even remove her scarf in my presence. Because I was segregated like that, my pastimes were biting my nails, scratching my forehead, plucking at the seven stitches in my forehead, staring at the light bulb until my eyes watered and singing carnival songs in an effort to stifle undesirable memories. Under such circumstances my already poor Hungarian, in the heart of Budapest, could only perish. The only Hungarian I heard was muffled voices in the distance, the radio or fights between neighbours. Or Pisti sticking his head into the pantry and shouting something that sounded Turkish. Or when I was fast asleep, I would hear Kriska's slurred voice mixed with the voices of strange men; and what they said made no sense. One day Kriska brought me a tray of steaming pumpkin rolls, waved them under my nose and asked: *Hány?* *Hány*, I thought, *hány* means how many. I was going to ask for five, but I couldn't remember how to say five, or four, or three, or anything. When she realised that my Hungarian was truly dangling by a thread, Kriska became alarmed; she had hardened her heart to me, however, she was a woman, and did not want me to

128

become completely alien to her. She soon discharged me and got me the job; she seemed to say something to the effect that I'd have to work like a slave to pay my room and board.

When *The Necklace of Plums*, a book of short stories by Hidegkuti István, came out, I was already familiar with some passages that the author himself had read at the club. On my way to the Bulgarian market, where I intended to buy a fan, I saw the book in a shop window and decided to buy it, after observing that a new book cost the same as a used fan. I read the stories while sweating buckets, because the pantry is a hothouse in summer, but I was enchanted nevertheless, I'm not sure whether because of the prose itself or because I had understood some eighty per cent of it, and was thus able to guess the rest. Before that book, all I had read in Hungarian were the daily minutes of the Belles-Lettres Club. But this reading was easier for me, as I had been present during the meetings and had studied them so often on the recorder. At the end of summer, I even bought an old portable typewriter and tried my hand at transcribing a few recordings to compare with the text of the minutes and assess my writing progress. I developed a taste for it and after a year my spelling mistakes were almost nonexistent. And I thought that if Kriska were to see my exercises she would have to be proud of her former student.

Although she still spared me few words, she ate dinner with me more often and drank her vermouth at home. I would thus finish my transcriptions before dinner, take the typed pages to the table and leave them there as if I had forgotten them, after coffee. I would wash my dishes and sit in the pantry, from where I could hear Kriska's Hungarian operettas. And if Pisti wasn't there, she would turn up the volume with each new aria and trill in unison with the soprano. When the music stopped, I would go to the living room, where, beside the lamp, I would find my work corrected in red pencil, under the bottle of vermouth. And I rejoiced to see that most of the mistakes were not mine, but those of the distinguished men of Hungarian letters, who, in an informal discussion or the heat of a debate, were also subject to grammatical slips. I would then copy the work out neatly and deliver it to the club secretary the following morning, together with the recordings. Old Puskás Sándor would glance about and, in the wink of an eye, pocket the wad of papers as if it were a bribe. He did not thank me, of course, nor did he look me in the face, somewhat embarrassed to receive his work ready and unblemished, freeing him from a day spent listening to and editing that babble. He grew so accustomed to this procedure that, if I appeared in his office without the transcriptions, he would glare at me and snarl: *Lusta vastagbörü*, lazy pachyderm. But it was not my fault if Kriska had her occasional relapses, stayed out late and arrived home in no state to be of help to me. Mind you, as a result of her tacit lessons, in a few more months I had absorbed the rules of the formal register and was able to touch up the Hungarian of the greatest writers in Hungary on my own. I worked relentlessly at this task, renounced all leisure activities, and even spent Sunday afternoons hunched over the material from the previous night. Like that spring Sunday when I was slogging away at the transcription of a conference on onomatopoeia, in which the Magyar language is known to be steeped. Some speakers, however, perhaps somewhat excessively, saw the sounds of nature in the etymology of all manner of words. And to back up their theories, they made strange noises, primitive phonemes, simulated animal sounds. And to boot, on all four recording channels, there was a metallic beating, *pléhek*, *pléhek*, and I had the task of giving written form to all these sounds. I also registered, with due corrections, interjections from the auditorium and arguments between panel members, as the topic was controversial, giving rise to protests, jeers and foul insults, and the higher the spirits, the lower the vernacular. I was exhausted when I finished the job, and while I rewound the last reel, and even after I removed the earphones, I could still hear *pléhek*, *pléhek*.

I went to the window and only then did I realise that the sound was Kriska, skating in front of the house. Spring appeared to be doing her good; she was flushed, wearing a short skirt, and that night, instead of frozen food, she served freshly prepared spaghetti Bolognese. She also made me open a bottle of Italian wine, which I only tasted, afraid I'd be billed at the end of the month. And before serving coffee, she took up the papers I had brought to the table and began to read them in front of me. I'm not sure if it was the Chianti, spring, or her own benevolence, but Kriska read my pages without blinking; a cigarette turned to smoke between her fingers and the red pencil remained untouched beside her plate. When she finished reading, she lowered her face and said: *Feddhetetlen*, impeccable. She said the word with a tremor in her voice and I saw her eyes well with tears. I realised that Kriska's heart had thawed again. And she probably imagined that I would turn my back on her as soon as I knew the entire Hungarian language. So I placed my hand over hers and said: I shall for ever be your humble and grateful disciple. With a tear still trickling down her cheek, she smiled and said: Keep talking, for God's sake. And I said: The best words I know emanated from you, they owe you their vigour and beauty. And she said: Just once more, I beseech you. And I said: My words shall be yours alone, to you I shall dedicate my days and nights. That was when Kriska said my accent was really funny.

For an immigrant, an accent may be a form of vengeance, a way of insulting the language that constrains him. In the language he does not esteem, he will mumble only the words necessary to his work and daily life, always the same words, not one more. And even these he shall forget at the end of his life, to return to the vocabulary of childhood. Just as the names of those around us are forgotten when the memory begins to lose water, as a swimming pool slowly drains away, as yesterday is forgotten while our deepest memories remain. But for one who had adopted a foreign tongue as if hand-picking his own mother, for one who had sought out and loved every last one of its words, the persistence of an accent was an unfair punishment. Sometimes I would be in bed with Kriska, praising her thick eyebrows or her naked belly, and suddenly it was as if I had tickled her: Stop, Kósta, for the love of God, stop, and she would double up with laughter. Where did I go wrong, what consonant? Stop, stop, Kósta, I beg you. I also experienced embarrassing situations with Pisti, notwithstanding my determination to impose my authority on him, now that I considered him more or less my stepson. I insisted on seeing his school results, went through his essays, and thought it absurd that secondary-school pupils did not know how to employ the personal infinitive. What pupils? I repeated: *Középiskola*, the word for secondary school. And Pisti: I don't understand. And me: *Középiskola*. Pisti: Again. Me: *Középiskola*, isn't that how you say it? No, idiot, it's *középiskola*, and the worst thing was, I couldn't tell the difference. I strove to speak such fastidious Hungarian that perhaps for this very reason it sometimes rang false. Perhaps a word here or there, pronounced with excessive zeal, stood out like a glass eye that was more realistic than the good eye. Just in case, I did not utter a word at the Belles-Lettres Club, although I was tempted. When revising the minutes, however, I no longer limited myself to correcting linguistic mistakes. Because even writers of the calibre of Hidegkuti István, for example, could not be inspired every single day. I had, on occasion, reluctantly transcribed in the minutes some rather banal observations coming from the mouths of refined intellectuals. And not infrequently they were reproduced in the monthly edition of the Belles-Lettres magazine, which circulated mostly in the academic arena. In order to preserve certain reputations, I began to take the liberty of replacing such drivel with spirited ideas of my own authorship. It was a risky game, because if my intervention were not to the person's liking, the club secretary would be blamed. And, although his negligence would be revealed, old Puskás would surely sacrifice me in order to save his own job. But those gentlemen of letters never complained about my words; on the contrary, they would occasionally recite them as if they were indeed theirs: As I was saying the other day . . . And they would glance furtively at old Puskás, who puffed right up and didn't glance in my direction, not even furtively. With abundant spare time on his hands, Puskás Sándor began spending time in the library, where he enjoyed growing prestige. During the public sessions on Saturdays, he sat at the table between such celebrities as the fiction writer Hidegkuti and the poet Kocsis Ferenc, and behind the scenes he was even greeted by the elusive Mr . . . . As for me, since Kriska no longer charged me room and board, I ended up subcontracting a Bulgarian sound technician to operate the recorder. And I installed myself in old Puskás' office, certain that he would not mind lending me his swivelling chair. There I answered the odd telephone call, read novels, essays, newspapers, articles on local politics, the cultural pages, sports pages, even the classifieds. And one day it occurred to me to publish an advertisement, offering my writing services for dissertations, theses, speeches and works of fiction, based at the Belles-Lettres Club. I'm not sure it was entirely ethical to use the club address for personal

135

ends, or even to do other work on the premises. I judged it unlikely, however, that the club members, sophisticated readers, would stoop to read classifieds. At any rate, to avoid any problems I signed the advertisement Puskás Sándor, club secretary. And I had the word *bizalomgerjesztö*, trustworthiness, printed in bold.

The advertisement ran in Sunday's *Magyar Hírlap*, and by Monday morning I had spoken to two clients: a young language and literature student and a retired public servant with purple hair. I quickly dispatched the public servant because she had requested a poem, something I had never written, and besides, she had a few screws loose; she intended to be the receiver of the poem, on embossed paper with the seal of the Belles-Lettres Club. The young man, on the other hand, commissioned a five-page essay on the Székely dialect. As the topic was not unfamiliar to me, I promised to deliver the essay in twenty-four hours for the price of five thousand forints, without a receipt. Possibly the most rudimentary of the Hungarian dialects, Székely is used in Eastern Transylvania. That was the opening line of my first essay in Hungarian, handwritten in a brand new notebook on old Puskás' ebony table. Used in Eastern Transylvania, Székely is possibly the most rudimentary of the Hungarian dialects. Of the Hungarian dialects, Székely, used in

Eastern Transylvania, is possibly the most rudimentary. Székely, possibly the most rudimentary of the Hungarian dialects . . . The afternoon drew to an end, the club closed its doors and I was getting nowhere in my work. I returned home disgruntled, refused dinner and shut myself in the pantry, which I still kept as a private office. I turned on the computer and electric heater and lit a cigarette. In Eastern Transylvania . . . I set the essay to one side and forced myself to resume my daily tasks, the earphones, the transcription of the recordings, the revision of the text. I prepared the minutes, and Kriska crooned in the bedroom, but I could not go to bed yet, my professional future was at stake. Of the Hungarian dialects, possibly the most rudimentary . . . As it happened, less than a month before, while queuing at the tobacconist's, an odd sort in front of me had asked for a packet of Facskë cigarettes. I corrected him: Excuse me, my good man, the correct pronunciation is *Fecske*. But he insisted: Facskë. I pointed to the advertisement right in front of him, showed him the drawing of the swallow, and spelled out the brand name, letter by letter: It's *Fecske*. Can't you read? And the man, grunting: Facskë. It's *Fecske*. Facskë. We might well have come to blows had the tobacconist not stepped in to settle the squabble; we were both absolutely correct, I with my unblemished Budapestian Hungarian, and he with

his legitimate Székelyland dialect. I ended up frater-
nising with the peasant, took him to a café on Czibor
Square, gave him four or five shots of firewater and
acquired a trick or two in his tongue. We then walked
through streets of Pest he didn't know, went bowling,
ate sausages, he ran riot in the sex shop and came out
saying tits, cunt and arsehole in dialect. We went to a
shopping centre, I insisted he ride the escalator, we
went into several boutiques, he bought sunglasses,
received a free cap with a slogan in English, we drank
beer on the panoramic terrace, but by now I was
growing sick of his manners. I paid my part of the bill,
got up, took the escalator down and he followed me.
He was embarrassing, raised his voice, said tits, cunt
and arsehole, and even in dialect everyone understood. I cut across the street, he caught up with me, I
jumped into a taxi, could still hear him saying: Facskë,
Facskë, and almost crushed his fingers closing the
door. As a result of that episode, however, I developed
an interest in the many Hungarian dialects. I picked
up some books at the library and compiled mountains
of information on the subject, never imagining that it
would come in handy so soon. But even if I had been
lacking in linguistic and anthropological knowledge, I
believed I had sufficient stylistic resources to fill pages
and pages of an undergraduate essay with panache.
Meanwhile, in Eastern Transylvania . . . I smoked and

smoked and tried to write about something else, an object at hand, the packet of cigarettes, for example. I jotted down a few lines inspired by the packet itself, gathered momentum, and off I went. I even began to enjoy myself, amused by the unusual appearance of my own writing. The sentences were mine, but they were not sentences. The words were mine, but they had a different weight. I wrote as if I were walking through my own house, but in water. It was as if my prose had taken the form of poetry. I did not know how to write poetry, yet I was writing a poem about swallows. I know it was poetry because it was untranslatable, except into the Székely dialect, where the word swallow, *facskë*, also sounds like the beating of wings, *fecske*. I finished the poem and read it over and over on the screen, in a low voice, in wonderment. And when I made out Kriska's silhouette through the smoke, I told her I was a happy man and would join her in bed in a jiffy. Kriska replied that the sun was shining outside and I looked like a madman. But no, I was actually biting my tongue, because I could not reveal that I was a writer in my native tongue. Nor would she believe me, were I to announce that I had become, simply, a poet in Hungarian.

I worked the sound desk during Saturday night lectures so Kriska wouldn't find out about the Bulgarian sound technician; she was bound to enquire as to what I was doing with my free time. And my free time I wiled away in the club secretary's office, awaiting clients interested in poetry. I kept my only poem, the one about the swallow, in the pocket of my navy-blue coat, handwritten on the embossed letterhead of the club. I hoped to sell it to the retired public servant who had commissioned it, and it was she I looked for when I craned my neck in the wings during Saturday night lectures. Especially during the presentations of Kocsis Ferenc, the distinguished poet, heartthrob of all the retired ladies with purple hair. Seeing them all together in the auditorium, however, I couldn't work out which one was mine. Dozens of elderly ladies waited for Kocsis Ferenc, open-mouthed, and chanted his poems in a chorus, as if he were an old-time pop singer. Even I knew the poems off by heart, as Kocsis Ferenc always repeated the same ones. And he would finish his reading with his all-time favourite, an epic poem that the old ladies declaimed in a crescendo, culminating with the line: *Egyetlen, érintetlen, lefordítha-tatlan!* I was under the impression that I had heard this line sometime in the distant past, even before learning to speak the language. Kocsis himself reminded me of a Hungarian poet I had seen in Brazil many years before. But beyond the marks of time, there was damage of another nature separating that lordly poet from this old man with lacklustre eyes. I pitied him on

Saturday nights because, except for the purple-headed women, he was not well received by the audience. At the mere mention of his presence, there would be a tut-tutting in the crowd. Irreverent remarks were shouted out in the pauses between lines, and people who were younger, or demanding like Kriska, would abandon the auditorium mid-recital. The other members of the panel would cast glances at one another, whisper, snigger, and Mr . . ., a fixture in the wings, would gesture to me to halt the recording, which I had already done. The atmosphere towards Kocsis Ferenc in the library was also unfriendly on weekdays, perhaps because Mr . . . was not particularly partial to him. Mr . . . wielded great influence within the Belles-Lettres Club, although he was a man of few words, without any published work of which I was aware at the time. He listened to everyone with interest, if not with patience, but when Kocsis Ferenc spoke, he looked at the ground and shook his head. It was enough to make the poet lose his way, and his already cloudy thoughts became inconclusive; his rare utterances were eliminated in the editing of the minutes. More recently, in fact, when he came to the club, he would only visit the library to sign the attendance register and would then wander aimlessly through the corridors. He talked to himself, counted syllables on his fingertips, and one day invaded the office huffing

141

and puffing. Paper, he needed paper urgently, and without a second thought I handed him the brand-new notebook I had bought for my future poems. He sat opposite me at the ebony table, in the chair reserved for my clients. He opened the notebook, took an old-fashioned pen out of his pocket, unscrewed the cap with difficulty, and his hand trembled and trembled as if it were writing frenetically, in the air. But no sooner had he set pen to paper than the trembling stopped, his hand became immobile and not a single word happened. Studying the poet's countenance, I saw beads of sweat in the furrows of his forehead. I saw yellow teeth and thought the poet was laughing, but it was a twitch of the mouth. Then his nerves gradually distended, his shoulders slumped, his entire body went limp, the pen slid from his hand and with a slack mouth, he said: I've lost it. He left the office slowly without saying another word; he had no reason to say anything and probably wasn't even sure who I was. At any rate, he had inaugurated my poetry notebook. He had left a black dot at the top of the first page, where he had jabbed the paper with his pen. And from that dot I wrote a line, then another, then one more. I read my three lines and was satisfied; perhaps they were the very words that Kocsis Ferenc had been chasing for years on end. The following day I wrote a new verse of three lines, which Kocsis would most certainly have liked to have written. I judged the three lines of the third day to be of a superior level, although vaguely reminiscent of Kocsis Ferenc's style. Every day from there on, a new verse would occur to me that was better than that of the previous day, and I filled my poetry notebook with lines that Kocsis Ferenc had never dreamed of writing. I imagined his astonishment when he set eyes on that poem, signed with his own name, and, overcome with emotion, I decided not to charge a fee for work that, at the end of the day, had cost me nothing. One morning I followed him at a distance through the corridors until I saw him enter the toilet. As we pissed side by side, I silently handed him the notebook with the long poem entitled *Titkos Háromsoros Versszakok, Secret Tercets*.

One does not learn the Magyar language from books. I beg your pardon? One does not learn the Magyar language from books, I repeated in Kriska's ear. It was to remind her of the first sentence she had said to me when we met for the first time at that same bookshop. Kriska was slow to catch on, then she whispered something or other that I barely heard, because I was trying to eavesdrop on a couple whispering behind me. In spite of the multitude of people present, an almost reverential atmosphere surrounded the launch of *Secret Tercets*. A string quartet was playing on the mezzanine and it was not easy to distinguish words in the murmuring of people clutching, exhibiting, fondling, leafing through and talking about the book in every corner. A film crew was filming a documentary about Kocsis Ferenc and the queue for autographs was not moving. Whenever an artist or glamorous woman arrived at the table, Kocsis would stand, hold out his hand, sit again, stand, hold out his hand, sit again, and so on over and over again so the scene could be filmed from a variety of angles. Ministers and senators would suddenly enter, official parties jumped the queue, the queue moved backwards and we ended up under the awning. We were getting rained on when I mutinied: It is inconceivable that a cultural event of this magnitude should become a pageant for the privileged. Kriska asked me to lower my voice, but the people around us nodded their heads in agreement. No, Fülemüle Krisztina, it is unjust that the true lovers of high literature should agonise in the dew. That night I felt my spoken Hungarian had reached perfection, perhaps ever so slightly nasal, like that of the old families of Buda, and several people came up to shake my hand. Come, Fülemüle Krisztina, enough of walking backwards among the rabble. I pulled her along by the arm and, shrugging off an insult or two, penetrated the bookshop all the way to the back, where I ran into a bunch of gorillas standing around the table. Poet, I cried, branding my copy, will you not honour me with an autograph? Cut! cried the film director in response. The reflectors were turned off and an arse-kisser addressed me: Who are you? Put your question to the poet himself, amorphous creature, I replied, and Kocsis Ferenc gestured for them to make way for me. I deposited my book on the table, which he took a long time to sign, his hand trembling against the white page. It is for Zsoze Kósta, I said. Do not tell me you have forgotten the name of your servant. For Zsoze Kósta, cordially yours, K., he wrote. I then took Kriska's copy from her hands: This is for my ladylove, Fülemüle Krisztina. I turned to the film crew: Please feel at liberty, good ladies and gentlemen, to film my lovely wife. Oh Kósta, said Kriska, but the reflectors came on and Kocsis Ferenc stood three times to greet her, then signed the book: For Fülemüle Krisztina, cordially yours, K. I had intended to enjoy the reception a little longer, listen to violins, taste drinks and canapés, but Kriska was restless and left the bookshop looking for a taxi. I convinced her that we should walk home, as the rain had ceased and it was the first fresh night of spring. Heading down Bozsik Avenue, with its birches in bloom, I was unable to resist reciting the first few pages of the book, which, armed with a pair of glasses, I pretended to read. I was certain that Kriska would delight in the tercets of the Ornithic Introit, in which the words copied the morning song of Hungarian birds. In fact, she listened in such silence that I decided to continue with the poem, at least until the Symphony of the Nymphomaniacs, with which I was sure to prise some malicious laughs from her. But she did not laugh, perhaps because a light rain had begun to fall again, forcing us to pick up our pace. And as we were walking fast, I automatically sped up my recital, to the detriment of the interpretation. When we were close to home the rain grew heavier and we sought shelter under a poplar. It was providential, because the poem was reaching its climax and beneath the poplar I was able to deliver it with the appropriate inflections. And with a lump in my throat I declaimed the final tercets of the Specular Crepuscule. I closed the book, drenched and almost coming apart in my hands, and asked Kriska: What do you think? So-so, she said. What do you mean, so-so? She looked at the street full of puddles, looked at the unyielding rain and decided: Let's go. Slipping off her heels, she took off, holding them in her hand. What do you mean, so-so? I asked as we arrived home, and Pisti, sprawled on the divan, smoking, complained about the time and said he was starving. Kriska went into the kitchen, and while I changed my clothes, I brooded over her so-so. What do you mean, so-so? I asked at the dinner table. It's an opinion, for heaven's sake. Opinion? What does a woman who makes her living reading fairy-tales to idiots know about literature? Kriska swallowed her food, took a sip of wine and went quiet. Do not take this amiss, my dear Kriska, but I can assure you that our Pisti is more sensitive to Kocsis Ferenc's poetry than you are. I opened the book and for Pisti's benefit recited the Rhapsody of the Diaspora, certainly the most exuberant of the tercets. What do you say, Pisti? And Pisti replied: mortiferous, an adjective used by young Hungarians to describe exceptional things, good or bad. Good or bad mortiferous? So-so mortiferous, said Pisti. I became incensed and spoke about the preface of the book, signed by Professor Buzanszky Zoltán; I spoke about highbrows in the autograph queue going into raptures over Kocsis Ferenc. Well, Kósta, there are those who appreciate the exotic, said Kriska. Exotic? What do you mean, exotic? Just that the poem doesn't seem Hungarian, Kósta. What are you saying? That the poem just doesn't seem Hungarian, Kósta. The words did not offend me as much as the candid manner in which Kriska enunciated them. And she continued: It's as if it were written with a foreign accent, Kósta. She almost sang this sentence, and it was what made me lose my head. I took my plate of spaghetti and flung it at the wall. The plate shattered, and the tangle of tomato, minced meat and much of the pasta, sticky because Kriska always

147

overcooked it, remained stuck to the wall. It was a brutal gesture, but not enough to placate me. So I went and looked her in the eye and shouted that I hated spaghetti Bolognese. A silence ensued until Pisti pointed at the wall and said: Mortiferous. Kriska got up, walked slowly into the kitchen, returned with a dustpan, broom, bucket of water and cloth, and it irritated me to see her squatting there, as if urinating, her dress still wet from the rain and dripping on the floor. She swept up the pieces, the food around her clogs, removed the thick gunk from the wall, went to the kitchen and came back with a sponge. She wiped the sponge across the wall in sweeping movements, deliberately spreading the red stain, and I understood that in that house I was no longer welcome.

My belongings fitted into a holdall. There were stars in the sky and I headed towards the city centre. Still far from the centre, however, I found a modest-looking hotel with the name Zakariás in iron letters over the door. I rang the bell at the counter and saw a price list indicating that the single-room rate was four thousand forints a day. I calculated that I could afford to stay there for more than a month, as Kocsis Ferenc had insisted on remunerating my services: two hundred thousand forints in hush money. I was about to ring the bell again when an old man appeared adjusting his braces. He asked for my documents in

atrocious English, said Mr Costa, Mr Costa, rummaged through a drawer, said yes, and told me they
had been waiting for me since Wednesday. He gave
me the key to 713 and a plastic card saying Mr Costa,
and underneath, Brazil. I became giddy, and looked
from the nametag to the old man, who told me the
meeting was on the underground floor. That was
when the penny dropped that the Zakariás Hotel in
Budapest was hosting the annual anonymous authors'
convention. I had never again contacted them, for
some reason feeling myself unworthy of them, and I
was moved to know that they always remembered me,
nevertheless. I went downstairs and, when I opened
the door at the end of the corridor, I found myself in a
windowless room, with rows of chairs from where
some thirty odd heads turned my way. I instantly
recognised those faces and shivered. I had not seen
them since Istanbul, I don't know how many years
before, and I was able to make out the passage of time
on each face, if on each face I paused a little. But
seeing all of those faces at once was frightening; it was
as if they had become decrepit at that exact instant.
Other faces that I remembered as geriatric were no
longer there, and, oblivious to my arrival, the man
standing at the microphone at the other end of the
room, neither young nor old, continued his reading;
this man did not belong to memory. He was so close

and present that in a room full of remote faces I hesitated to recognise him. The text he was reading in Hungarian was not unknown to me, although I had not accompanied it from the beginning. I remembered the words, but did not understand their circumstances, as if I was in a familiar house unable to remember what it was like on the outside. With great effort I more or less managed to recompose the story, which appeared to be about a hunchbacked psychoanalyst, in a story called, if I am not mistaken, 'Interrogating Rabbits'. And the person reading it was none other than Mr . . . in a hoarse voice that I was not certain I had heard before. It was a voice appropriate to a story full of macabre events, to which the audience, plugged into earphones, did not react. But a little further along, in a banal passage, they went oh, because not even the most quick-witted interpreter can handle Hungarian in simultaneous translation. Half a dozen interpreters were installed with their equipment in the last row, where I also sat so as not to disrupt the session. And when Mr . . . finished reading the story, I heard the reverberation of its tragic end for a minute in six different languages. Then the audience erupted into applause, followed by a great deal of laughter after Mr . . . revealed the name of the supposed author, Hidegkuti István, and listed off the literary prizes awarded to the acclaimed writer. I also clapped,

out of politeness, because in all truth the prose of
Hidegkuti, or Mr . . ., did not impress me. In fact, after
a certain point I had stopped paying attention, because
the story was somewhat verbose and I was itching to
get my hands on that microphone. But Mr . . . did not
intend to give it up so soon. Tossing back his black
hair, he launched into passages from his novels, essays
and plays, works attributed to the most eclectic range
of authors, and that there was not one poet among
them was comforting. Almost aphonic, he ended his
presentation with a collection of generous reviews of the
same works, which he had published in the press under
the signature of the venerable Professor Buzanszky
Zoltán, bringing the audience to a standing ovation.
And before anyone else could take control of the
microphone, I whipped my book from my bag and
strode across the room. I positioned myself beside
Mr . . ., whose nametag read: Mr . . ., Hungary, and
waited for him to pile his leather-bound books against
his chest. Only then did he see me; recognising me, he
almost dropped his pile of books. Steadying them with
his chin, he looked down his nose at me, although he
was much shorter than I. He sat on a side chair,
cluttered up another two with his stacks of books,
and when he saw me holding a disintegrating wet
paperback that was missing its cover, he leaned back
in his seat, legs apart. He stiffened, however, when I

introduced *Secret Tercets*, a poem I had authored in the name of the distinguished Kocsis Ferenc, with a preface from the venerable Professor Buzanszky Zoltán. I had intended to but did not read the preface, an authentic Buzanszky, whose infinitely superior style might have humiliated Mr . . . . I preferred to humiliate him with poetry, an art of which he was ignorant, and which would make him suffer much more as he would not know where it hurt. I declaimed the lines slowly; there were words I almost spelled out, for the pleasure of seeing him squirm in his chair. I paused for long seconds, silences that only poets allow themselves, and he lowered his head, glanced sideways at his piles of books, and even piled them up on his lap as if about to leave. But I had the upper hand; with my tercets on the tip of my tongue, I was declaiming the Apotheosis of the Poets and knew he would remain seated until the end. I barely concerned myself with the rest of the audience, some wiping away tears, others thoroughly amused, yet others staring at the interpreters, who appeared to be tearing their hair out at the back of the room. Faced with the impossible task of translating a Hungarian poem, I imagine each one said whatever sprang to mind. I was performing for the benefit of Mr . . ., and I bowed to him at the end of the poem, amidst boos and bravos. I pranced across the room, found the lift out of order, and took off up

152

the stairs with a blast that began to cool after the third flight. It took me hours to reach the seventh floor with my holdall, panting and leaning against the walls for support. I entered the room feeling queasy, went to the toilet and stuck a finger down my throat, but I had not eaten, there was nothing in me to vomit. I lay down, missing Kriska, couldn't get a phone line out. I thought of going home, but had no strength, no keys, my head spun, the poem spun in my head and I had had enough of poems. Luckily it was late at night, and a tenuous light was beginning to filter through the cracks in the shutters when there was a knock at my door. Still dizzy, I got up, certain it was breakfast, and I could have hugged the room-service waiter and kissed his cheeks; I was famished and could have swallowed seven pumpkin rolls without even chewing them. But in the corridor a thickset man introduced himself as Federal Police agent Grosics. He asked if I was Mr Zsoze Kósta, employee of the Belles-Lettres Club, and asked to see my passport. He fiddled with it and enquired whether I was perchance in possession of any other papers, a permanent visa, a work permit, making me see that my situation in the country was completely illegal. He requested my plane ticket, but I had not kept it, as I had come to Budapest on a one-way ticket. He instructed me to contact my embassy if I did not have the money for the return trip; I had forty-eight hours in which to leave Hungary once and for all.

I wandered aimlessly through the streets of Pest with my holdall until the airline opened its doors. The employee who served me was grappling with Hungarian, but with a little French I helped her book my departure on the Sunday afternoon flight. Then I realised with a start that I had spoken French. And I was even more startled to realise that I was resigned, then relieved, then almost happy to be saying goodbye to the Hungarian language. Guanabara, I murmured, *goiabada*, Pão de Açúcar. I said *arrivederci*, spoke German in the middle of the street, and even remembered a few words of Turkish. I tried out words here and there from languages of my acquaintance, a little like the newly single revisit old girlfriends. I addressed the taxi driver in English, letting him think I was an unsuspecting foreigner, while he drove about in circles on his way to Tóth Street. The forints I had left, although no great fortune, I had no way of spending in a day and a half in Budapest. I could even have headed straight for the airport to roam around, have a few drinks, go to the duty-free shop, snooze a little in the departure lounge, if I did not have to say goodbye to Kriska and leave her with better memories than a plate flung against the wall. But as the taxi turned into our street, I caught sight of the cul-de-sac of terraced houses from afar, and among the dozens of identical roofs, I identified the pitched roof that had sheltered me for so many years. And I remembered Kriska greeting me at the doorstep the first time we met: Zsoze Kósta ... Zsoze Kósta ... In thought I answered: There I am arriving almost, beautiful, white, Fecske cigarettes, table, coffee, skates, bicycle, window, shuttlecock, happiness, one, two, three, nine, ten, and I came to my senses; learning Hungarian had been child's play, the difficult part would be erasing it from my mind. And I shuddered to think that soon, far from Kriska and her land, all of the words in the Hungarian language would be as much use to me as leftover coins in the pockets of return travellers. Turning to the taxi driver, I said: You can leave me on the right, after the old truck, at number 84. And he eyed me warily, not because I was suddenly speaking Hungarian, but because I had said something so pedestrian in a constricted voice. It's me, I said quietly on the intercom, and after a time Pisti buzzed the gate open. I found the house door open, the living room empty and glanced at the wall, which at first sight looked unscathed. Close up, however, a few red and brown residues were visible on the rough surface. Sitting on the bed, with the bedroom windows closed and the oblique light of the lampshade accentuating her cheekbones, Kriska had an Oriental air about her. I

155

approached her cautiously, sat beside her, and after a time I took her hand in mine. She said nothing, nor did I know what to say. My body relaxed, I leant over, burying my face in her lap, and was suddenly gripped by a spasm, a feeling of being strangled, a violent gasping; I sobbed as a pig grunts, and was slow to understand what was happening to me. My eyes flooded over on to my cheeks, my whole face, Kriska's nightie; I sucked Kriska's nightie to confirm the taste of my tears. And Kriska said: It's nothing, it's nothing, it's over, it's over, thinking I was crying because of the damage to the wall. One day we'll paint over it, she said, and ran her fingertips over my bald patch, saying: Sleep, sleep, sleep, sleep. I awoke to Kriska flinging open the bedroom window; the sun was shining outside. She was wearing shorts and said she had sent Pisti to spend the weekend with his father. She opened my bag, emptied my wadded-up clothes on the bed and handed me my jeans to put on. And she lent me one of Pisti's shirts, green and white, with the number 9 of the Ferencváros' centre forward, which made me look pot-bellied. She had prepared a basket of wine and cheese and had planned an afternoon for us on Margit Island.

It was blustery on Margit Island, the picnic blanket lifted up at the corners, the paper napkins flew away and Kriska laughed. Her straw hat went flying and she pointed at my head, my thinning hair flapping in the wind, and laughed herself silly. We went home to change clothes, she ironed my navy-blue suit and put on a pink two-piece. It was Saturday night, but there was no way I was going to the club. Luckily she suggested we go dancing, as there was nothing wrong with missing work once in one's life, besides which . . . She was going to say, besides which, we would be spared Kocsis Ferenc's tercets. Besides which, it is the anniversary of our engagement, she improvised. We went to the revolving disco, danced our feet off, ate a pizza in the old city and I took a bottle of Tokay home from the restaurant. We walked with our arms around one another, sort of sideways; it was extremely windy on the bridge and the Danube was choppy. We drank the Tokay on her divan, singing the heart-rending ballad of Bluebeard's daughter as a duet. She undressed in the bedroom with the light off and said: Come. I lay on top of her, and even in the dark, I could see the expression on her face. I liked seeing her like that, distressed, her eyes rolling, as if she did not know where I was. When she fell asleep, I tried to reanimate her. I shook her, asked her to say something. What thing? Anything. We'll paint it tomorrow . . . was what she mumbled. I remained wide awake, watching the luminous hands of the alarm clock. I smoked the last of my cigarettes, found a packet on Kriska's desk and finished them off as well. At midday I got up, showered and dressed. Kriska was sleeping completely naked, and in the half-light she had the same body as when I had met her. I picked up my clothes from the floor, shoved them back into my holdall and closed it. I opened it again, zipped and unzipped it several times, because waking Kriska up with a metallic sound seemed more honest than calling her sweetly by her name. Kriska switched on the lamp, leapt from the bed, looked at the bag, looked at me, looked at the bag, looked at me, and I said farewell. I told her I was going to Rio de Janeiro, Brazil, that was all I could say. She stared at me, but I was not going to tell her that I had been thrown out of the country. I was not going to tell her about a police agent who had surprised me at daybreak in an obscure hotel, undoubtedly following up an anonymous report. I could not reveal the name of the anonymous writer, envious of my poetry, who I had challenged during a secret meeting of anonymous writers. And nothing in the world would make me confess that I was also an anonymous writer, especially the author of a book of poetry which, to top it all off, she considered so-so. I remained motionless, letting her think whatever she wanted, and I expected her to spit in my mouth and claw my face, then dig her fingernails into my eyes and rip them from their sockets, and I would bear it all. Kriska, however, did not lift a finger, preferring not to touch me. She took a deep breath, opened her mouth to say something, and I felt that with one word she would do me greater damage. With a single word Kriska would cover me with shame, cripple me, make me hobble with regret for the rest of my life. The word was poised on her unsteady lips; it must have been a word she had never dared utter. It must have been an archaic word, derived from the voice of a nocturnal bird, a word so atrocious it had fallen into disuse. It must have been the only word I did not know in the entire Magyar vocabulary; it must have been a stupendous word. Unable to contain myself, I begged her: Speak! Kriska did not speak. She expelled all of the air in her lungs, shook her head, went back to bed, pulled up the covers, rolled on to her side and switched off the lamp.

To the sound of a peaceful sea

THE EARLY MORNINGS WERE ideal for walks along the seafront, preferably in thick mist, to the sound of a peaceful sea. Only the headlights of the cars on the avenue could be seen. No one honked; no one honks at the invisible. And I moved at a rhythmic pace, occasionally speeding up because I didn't like it when people pulled up alongside me. No sooner had walkers heading the other way appeared than they had already passed, and with them, scattered words, pieces of words. Later the fog would begin to thin, the clouds lifting off the mountains; it was the city wanting to show its skin. Nevertheless, the people I came across, no matter how much they laughed and swung their bodies, did not look at home in that environment. Sometimes I saw them as film extras, walking to and fro or riding along the bicycle path at the director's orders. And the girls on skates were professionals, the street kids were paid, behind the steering wheels of cars were stuntmen, driving like animals down the avenue. I think I had preserved a photographic memory of the city, and now everything that moved over it struck me as an artifice. Finally, I would sit on a bench near the water's edge and watch the boats; even the ocean, in my memory, was on the verge of stagnation. But my seclusion never lasted long, as someone with nothing better to do would always end up sitting next to me. And he would strike up a conversation, not suspecting that meddling in my ears at that moment was akin to stopping me from breathing. He would touch my shoulder, my knee, no doubt thinking I was someone else, alluding to events I had supposedly witnessed, mentioning people he presumed to be close to me. Or he would be carrying a newspaper to comment on the headlines, which referred to facts and names that also meant nothing to me. They caught those butchers, d'ya see? And with the back of his hand the fellow would tap a dark photo in a newspaper with smudged letters. Look at the butchers, and he would show me the photograph of two bodies lying on the asphalt, one black and one mulatto. I would look at the photo, glance back at the beach, the girls playing volleyball, look back at the photo, a fat black man and a tall mulatto, decapitated. The butchers from the dairy, remember? Of course you remember, don't you? There they are. I needed time to catch up on events, and on my first night in Rio I had gone out to eavesdrop on conversations in the street without understanding what they were about, finally stopping at a juice bar full of young people. There, for a few seconds, I felt as if I had disembarked in a country whose language I did not know, which for me was always a nice feeling, as if life were starting from scratch. I soon recognised the Brazilian words, but even so, it was almost a new language I was hearing, not because of new slang, lexical errors or grammatical confusion. What caught my attention was actually a new resonance: there was a metabolism in the spoken language that perhaps only rusty ears were able to pick up. Like a different song, which a traveller might stumble across when suddenly opening the door of a room after a long absence. And at the juice bar I was making my longest journey of all, because there were years and years of distance between my language as I remembered it and that which I was now hearing, at once distressed and enraptured. Thus, without meaning to, I leant against the counter, sidled up to two more talkative lads, already watching them out of the corner of my eye, and this must have bothered them, because suddenly they both went quiet and confronted me. They were muscular young men with shaved heads and abundant tattoos, one with reptiles slithering up his arms, the other with what looked like hieroglyphics scattered across his bare chest. They chewed sandwiches with their mouths open and looked at me with disdain; who knows, maybe they thought I was a poof. I played innocent, looked at the fruit on display in the shop, walked out slowly, sensed boots walking behind me, and speeded up. Close to the corner I thought they had lost interest in me, and they were in fact standing quietly next to a motorbike when I looked back. And it was undoubtedly this look backwards that reincited them; they must have been the sort of skinhead that goes in for a bit of queer bashing. I heard the roar of the motorbike, turned down a one-way street and took off running, knowing it was useless, because they came the wrong way down the street and would grab me whenever they wanted. I turned left again into a street that was even darker, and ran another block with the motorbike right behind me, close to the kerb. I grew tired, dropped my pace, and they came in fits and starts, accelerating and braking, the loose exhaust pipe back-firing; their intention was to frazzle my nerves. So I stopped short and drew in my shoulders, waiting for them to jump on me and get it over with quickly. They passed me, drove the bike on to the pavement a little further on and got off. The driver squatted down to have a look at the engine and his mate looked in my direction. He came towards me with a cigarette in his mouth and made a gesture with his fingers, asking for a light. I patted my pocket where I usually carried cigarettes; it was empty, but he continued advancing until he was practically leaning against me. He was one hand taller than me; my eyes were level with his chest, and for a few moments I imagined I could decipher the hieroglyphics tattooed there. Then my eyes met his eyes staring at me, and they were feminine eyes, very black; I knew those eyes, Joaquim. Yes, it was my son, and I barely managed to stop myself from uttering his name; if I smiled at him and held out my arms, if I gave him a paternal hug, perhaps he would not understand. Or perhaps he had known from the start that I was his father, and that was why he was looking at me like that, why he had me trapped against the wall. He made a fist, drew back his arm, and I think he was going to get me in the liver, when I heard voices beside me. People started coming out of the wall, throngs and throngs of people came out of that black hole, which was the back door of a cinema. I mingled with the crowd, joined the people flocking towards the avenue, passed in front of the cinema, bars, a chemist's, a newsstand, galloped off between the cars and entered the hotel.

Perhaps because I had given up smoking, I was able to go from Leblon to Copacabana, there and back, there and back, from daybreak until early afternoon. I would arrive at the hotel feeling hungry, go to my room, order sandwiches, which took a long time to arrive, and the room-service waiters rejected the forints I offered them as tips. The manager was also suspicious of me, because after a week I still hadn't settled my bill. I had paid a visit to the bank and my account didn't exist any more, nor had anyone ever heard of Cunha & Costa Cultural Agency. As for Álvaro, I heard he had set himself up in Brasilia and was working on the staff of a politician who was a relative of his. I got the phone number of the office and an employee took my message, but Álvaro did not return my call. He no doubt thought I was looking for a job in Brasilia as well, when all I wanted was a quick settling of accounts: he definitely owed me some money. I called again a few days later from the hotel reception desk, and in front of the manager I gave the woman from the office an upbraiding. With the harsh accent I had brought from Hungary, I said I had friends in the press, threatened to create a scandal, a politician's henchman owed me almost one million dollars, and there I was in an embarrassing situation at the Plaza Hotel. Not even after that did Álvaro take my call, but I did gain some credibility with the manager. I gained time to think of a course of action; the politician, for example, might be interested in an autobiography. Propped up in bed, I scribbled on the hotel airmail paper, and what came out of me was not even words, but crude figures, childish drawings. And I wondered what my destiny might have been if, instead of being taught to read and write, I had been presented only with art books during my childhood. Then I imagined anonymous, illiterate painters, who would work in secret on the canvases of the great masters of painting. These painters would be pampered, eat only the most exquisite food and have silent lovers, but above all they would love seeing their works of genius signed by the great masters, displayed in museums the world over. And they would be reciprocally grateful, calling one another every day, each concerned with the health of the other, and the longevity of the masters would match the fecundity of their artists' inspiration. I burned the midnight oil musing over these things and drawing my animals, waiting for the early mornings ideal for walks. And one day, in Copacabana, passing in front of the building where the agency had been, I crossed the avenue on an impulse, greeted the guard and took the lift. There was now a dental surgery in the Cunha & Costa offices, and the receptionist asked if I had an appointment. I spotted the door at the back of the reception area, barged into my former room, and bent over a Formica-topped workbench was a prosthodontist, who almost fell off his chair when he saw me; he thought it was a hold-up and offered me some plaster mouths with gold teeth. But when he understood I had come in peace, that I only wanted to know where my desk had got to, he became enraged and rushed into the corridor in his white coat shouting for security. I left the building disillusioned; it would be impossible for me to retrieve the books I had kept under lock and key in my desk drawer. I had taken it into my head that, if I were to manually copy them one by one, I would regain the hand for writing novels to order. I would open an agency that was mine alone, become a millionaire, maybe even buy an entire floor of the Plaza Hotel. I thought of calling Brasilia, but Álvaro wouldn't have kept my paraphernalia. At the most he would have a copy of *The Gynographer*, and I wanted nothing to do with *The Gynographer*. Strolling through the shops in Copacabana, however, a bookshop window full of mustard-coloured books caught my eye. I drew closer, and perhaps the reflection of the sun on the glass was playing tricks with the colours, because the books turned to a shade of ochre with green letters. A little closer, and the title *The Gynographer*, in lilac gothic letters on the covers of the cinnamon-coloured books, was almost clear. But when I reached the bookshop the book was navy-blue and called *The Hypnologist*. I went in, saw a variety of books displayed on the tables, did the rounds of the shelves purely out of curiosity, and ran into the owner of the bookshop: *The Gynographer*, please. What was that? *The Gynographer*. You must be mistaken. We've got *The Hypnologist*, which has already sold more than a hundred thousand copies. I insisted: *The Gynographer*. He asked if it was a technical book, had never heard of anything like it. The liar; I remembered him, he'd made a fortune with my novel. He agreed to look it up on a computer, asked if the word was spelled g – u – y, and said: Guide to Guyana . . . gymnastics manual . . . the Gypsies . . . there's no listing for gynographer. Do you have the name of the author by any chance? Kaspar Krabbe? K – r – a – b – b – e? Krabbe . . . Krabbe . . . Kaspar . . . there's no listing for Kaspar Krabbe either. The publisher by any chance?

I found the envelope stuffed under the door when I entered the room. It contained a card from the general management of the Plaza Hotel, reminding me that I had been there for 100 days, and a bill I didn't even want to look at. I had begun to believe they had forgotten me, not least because the orders I placed with room service didn't arrive any more. As the manager had not come looking for me again either, I had assumed that my name, together with room 707, had been deleted from the memory of the hotel computer. Messengers turned their backs on me, porters did not open doors for me and perhaps the reception staff did not really understand who this guest was, what wretched room it was that he entered and left every day. But from that point on I thought it wise to suspend my outings. Walks, only in the bedroom, and I had nothing else to do all day long. I had already scribbled on all the writing paper, and drawing no longer appealed to me. I only turned on the television once, absent-mindedly, but I turned it off as soon as I heard a jittery TV news jingle. I did not use the telephone, nor did I switch on my lamp any more: 707 was always in the dark. I was no trouble for the maids, there were no clothes to wash, I went about naked and the do-not-disturb card was always on the door handle. I ate at odd times, sometimes a chicken drumstick, vegetables, sometimes rice, sometimes a hunk of bread with the scrapings of stroganoff sauce. Depending on the trays my neighbours left in the corridor, sometimes I even feasted on a bit of French cheese and half a glass of wine with a lipstick mark on the rim. And one night I was taking it easy, sipping some slightly watery whisky, when the telephone began to ring. It rang some ten times in a row, stopped, started again, and I even thought it might be Álvaro, but no one rings like that to settle a debt. It must have been the general management of the Plaza Hotels, because we were entering peak season, full capacity, we're sorry, sir, but an Argentinian couple have just arrived, we need to make 707 available, but I was not

170

about to answer that call and played dead. The night progressed, and I ended up getting used to that ringing, its intermittency; I already knew the last ring of a series, counted to seven and guessed the beginning of the next series. The sound that had irritated me just moments before slowly pacified me, and lulled by it, I fell asleep, as one who lives next to a railway must fall asleep. And just as this person must wake with a start in the middle of a night on which the train doesn't pass, I leapt out of bed when the telephone went silent. Without it I was more vulnerable; soon, soon, someone would come and bang on the door, a federal agent would burst into the room. I took my suit out of my holdall, dressed quickly, and decided to stay a step ahead of my adversary, going downstairs to meet him. In a dark suit and tie, I felt able to negotiate with anyone on an equal footing. I could ask the manager for a few days' grace to find another hotel, claim the right to at least one night's sleep, perhaps even ask them to keep calling me regularly until daybreak. Downstairs, however, there was only a night porter I did not recognise, who wished me good evening. I reached the street, breathed fresh air, went to have a look at the sea, and was sorry I had not discovered sooner the pleasure of strolling during those hours in which no one goes out on foot any more for fear of delinquents. As such, the beach promenade was all mine, not even the delinquents put in an appearance, and I could have tap-danced along it, should the fancy have taken me. I went to the end of Arpoador, returned to the lookout in Leblon, roamed through the neighbourhood, and before I knew it I was arriving at my old address. I stole away, headed for the hotel, but I must have lost my bearings, because after wandering around a bit I ended up again in front of the building where I had lived with Vanda. The third time I passed through, I came across a familiar face and hid behind a low wall. It was the night watchman, who was smoking outside the sentry box, looking upwards. There wasn't a single light on in the flats, but a tiny flame appeared in a seventh-floor window: someone was smoking in Vanda's room. He would take three or four deep puffs in a row and flick the butt down below, where the watchman would light another from the butt of the first. And the sun was already beginning to rise behind the building, the watchman looking at the sky, the flame glowing in the dark room, when I heard the squealing of tyres and was caught in the beam of two headlights; I was in the garage entrance. I flattened myself against the wall and a 4 × 4 came down the driveway, braking next to me; I was next to the driver's window and felt I was being observed from the inside. But I could see nothing through the black glass; the only thing I saw in that mirror was myself, the bags under my eyes, my unshaven face, my suit all crumpled. The car horn sounded and the garage door creaked open. The car dipped into the underground garage, the watchman slipped into the sentry box and Vanda's blinds were already down.

It was broad daylight when I zoomed through the hotel reception area, and no sooner had I reached my door when the telephone rang. Something told me that this time I should answer it, it was good news, it was good news. It was a turnaround in my fortune, I knew it was, I had this hunch, but meanwhile I was having a hard time getting the door open. I swiped the magnetic card through the lock and nothing, a little red light came on, the telephone ringing, it was a turnaround in my fortune. The telephone went quiet, I counted to seven, but only on thirteen did it start ringing again, I must have been counting too fast. I swiped and re-swiped the card, shook the door, pushed the latch, and only then did I realise the card was upside down. Green light, a turnaround, I flung myself into the room, the telephone went quiet, I counted to twenty, hello! Mr Zsoze Kósta? *Természetesen*! I confirmed. Praise the Lord! said the man, introducing himself as the Hungarian Consul. He had already gone through every Costa José in the telephone directory, and had been investigating the city's hotels since the previous night. Please be so kind, I said, as not to deprive me of hearing your blessed language, noting that my Hungarian prosody was still intact. But persisting in his horrendous Portuguese, the Consul asked me if I had perchance heard of Lantos, Lorant & Budai. Yes, of course, Lantos, Lorant & Budai, the great Hungarian booksellers, publishers of the country's most prominent authors, including the distinguished poet Kocsis Ferenc. The Consul said he was in possession of a Rio-Budapest plane ticket, issued in my name by Lantos, Lorant & Budai. Rio-Budapest? In my name? You jest, surely? An entry visa to the country, with the right to permanent residency, would also be granted to me at the Consulate. Ticket to Budapest, permanent visa, now it was clear: pressured by his publishers to repeat the runaway success of *Secret Tercets*, Kocsis Ferenc had confessed his poetic impairment. Also eager, however, for renewed glory, he had suggested behind closed doors that the abnegated poet Zsoze Kósta be imported from Brazil. Via Milan, said the Consul, I could leave that very night. I said I would see, I had a few things to tend to in Rio, pending affairs; I asked if the ticket was first class, but my head was already lifting off, my thoughts came in verses.

Written that book

THE IRIDESCENT COVER, I didn't understand the colour of that cover, the title *Budapest*, I didn't understand the name Zsoze Kósta printed there, I hadn't written that book. I didn't know what was going on, that crowd around me, I had nothing to do with it all. I wanted to return the book, but didn't know to whom, I had received it from Lantos, Lorant & Budai and gone blind. The reflectors dazzled me, it was Duna Televízió, I didn't understand that Duna Televízió, I needed to get out of there, the customs doors closed behind me. I looked at the airport signs, and through the glass some people were watching me, waving at me with books with iridescent covers. And I saw Pisti's smiling face, Pisti who never smiled, and the woman beside him with a small video camera looked like Kriska, but it

wasn't, it was, it wasn't, it was, but she was different.
A little further off, the person smiling at me was
Mr . . ., I had never seen those dark gums. And I
looked at Pisti, looked at Mr . . ., their thin bodies,
enormous heads, black hair, I couldn't understand
how the two of them suddenly looked so alike. I
sought Kriska's gaze, but her left eye was closed, the
right hidden behind the video camera, and I couldn't
get my head around the idea that she had once slept
with that guy. When she later assured me that he
was a good-hearted man, I listened in silence, I
couldn't tell Kriska her ex-husband was a bastard.
But at that time I still didn't understand a thing, it
had been a long journey, I had drunk wine, taken
sedatives. I was bewildered, my body swayed, reeled
to one side, my eyes were red, my body reeled to
the other side. I finally stood up straight, looked
straight ahead, my pupils were dilated, and Kriska's
half-covered face seemed round, I thought she had
put on a lot of weight. And when I understood that
she was pregnant, I began to shake all over, my lips
twitched, I became paralysed. Somewhat cross-eyed
and with a crooked mouth I froze, because Kriska
paused the video to rush to the baby, who had burst
into tears. When she wasn't breast-feeding, she liked
to show her videos, the shaky images, the restless
zoom; there was my scene at the airport, the child in

176

the maternity ward, I was supposed to have filmed the birth, but at the time I felt ill and left the delivery room. And when she wasn't watching a video or nursing the boy, Kriska read the book. She never tired of reading the book, now that she was on maternity leave, and had already read it aloud some thirty times. Truly incredible, she said, and looked at me in admiration, and made comments, pumpkin bread, where did you come up with this? Choir of ventriloquists, truly incredible, and this city Rio de Janeiro, these beaches, all these people walking nowhere at all, and this woman Vanda, where did you come up with this? Truly incredible, truly incredible, and I felt the blood rushing to my head. And to top it off she kept telling me her ex-husband had a heart of gold, he had become concerned when he learned of her state through Pisti, and had told Pisti to reassure his mother that he would spare no ingenuity or resources to bring her man back to Budapest. Naive, Kriska had been moved to tears, for few ex-husbands know how to be so altruistic, and she made Pisti relay to his father her profound gratitude. Meanwhile, the bastard was writing the book. He was falsifying my vocabulary, my thoughts and fancies, the bastard was inventing my autobiographical novel. And just as he had forged my handwriting on his manuscript, the story he had imagined was so close to mine that it sometimes seemed more authentic than if I had written it myself. It was as if he had printed colours on a film I remembered in black-and-white, oh, Kósta, this New Year's Eve party, this song about Egypt, this hairless German, I couldn't bear to hear it any more. And one night, in bed, I jumped on Kriska, threw the book across the room, held her by her hair, and remained like that, panting. I am not the author of my book, I wanted to tell her, but my voice wouldn't come out of my mouth, and when it did, it was to say: You are all I have. And Kriska whispered: Not today; the boy was sleeping there in the cot next to the bed, because he had to be breast-fed every half-hour. I am not the author of my book, I apologised at the Belles-Lettres Club, but everyone made a fuss of me and pretended not to hear, perhaps because, as the saying goes, I was mentioning rope in the house of the hanged. And the eminent poet Kocsis Ferenc, on the occasion of the sumptuous launch of Budapest, made a point of publicly greeting me in the Lantos, Lorant & Budai bookshop. He good-humouredly lamented that his *Secret Tercets* had not in fact sprung from the fanciful quill of Zsoze Kósta, making the crowd laugh. I am not the author of my book, I added, eliciting peals of laughter from the crowd. It was not a joke, but my statement was published as such the following day, with a photo on the cover of the *Magyar Hírlap*, and Lantos, Lorant & Budai called to say that the first edition had sold out in the bookshops. Commoners stopped me in the street, asked me to autograph their copies of the book, and with a numb hand I wrote dedications that were strange to me. Strange articles with my name on them appeared in the press almost every day. I was received in Parliament, dined at the Archbishop's Palace, at the University of Pécs I was made an honorary doctor, a title I received with a pompous speech, which appeared in my pocket goodness knows how. My footsteps grew slow, I went wherever they led me, already knowing what awaited me; it was as if my book was still being written. I still tried to speak off the cuff in lectures, and had the odd flash of spirit, but my readers already knew them all. I dreamed up preposterous words, back-to-front sentences, a fucking hell out of the blue, but no sooner had I opened my mouth, than some exhibitionist in the audience beat me to it. It was tedious, it was very sad, I could have pulled down my pants in the centre of the city and no one would have been surprised. Luckily, I still had my dreams, and in dreams I was always on a bridge over the Danube, in the dead of the night, staring at its leaden waters. And I would lift my feet off the ground and balance on my stomach on the parapet, overjoyed because I knew I could, at any moment, give my story a conclusion no one had foreseen. I dallied, enjoying that omnipotence, and with my dallying the sun would rise, the water would take on hues of green, and I soon found myself with restricted movements again. Police officers, firemen, paramedics and passers-by would grab me: Do not commit such madness, Illustrious Writer Zsoze Kósta, have faith in God, Illustrious Writer Zsoze Kósta. A priest, a rabbi, a gypsy, each would pull me in a different direction, probably wanting to appear in the book. I struggled to free myself, trying to disentangle myself from that mob, and awoke twisted up in the bed sheets, relieved to find myself beside Kriska, who had at least been in the book from the start. And on the first day of spring, observing Kriska's walk, I sensed that she had recovered from the pregnancy. She sang songs from other springs all afternoon, lulled the child to sleep in Pisti's room in the evening, bathed, and lay down beside me in a silk nightie. And asked me to read the book. What? The book. I would not read a book that was not mine; I would not subject myself to such humiliation. And she was not overly insistent, perhaps because she knew that sooner or later I would do as she wanted. She merely rested the book on my chest and lay there, inert. I picked it up, its pages came out in my hands; I didn't understand why I should have to read that jumble of words she had already read a thousand times. But a literary work must have nuances, said Kriska, which can only be perceived through the author's voice. Unwittingly, she was giving me an opportunity to provide her with definitive evidence that I could not be the author of a book with my name on its cover. I threatened to tear my name from that already somewhat grubby, unctuous cover, but when I saw Kriska's placid smile, her droopy eyes, her almost transparent skin, I was loath to hurt her. She would undoubtedly prefer to go on imagining it was my book she carried forever clasped to her bosom. It was very flattering for her that such a celebrated author, considered by the venerable Buzanszky Zoltán as the last purist of Hungarian literature, was this wild fellow whom she had initiated into the language. So I put on my glasses, opened the book and began: It should be against the law to mock someone who tries his luck . . . Slowly, Kósta, slow down, and the first few pages were hard to get through. I struggled with the punctuation, ran out of breath in the middle of sentences; it was like reading a text I really had written, but with dislocated words. It was like reading a life parallel to my own, and when speaking in

181

the first person, through a character parallel to me, I stammered. But after I learned to distance myself from the me in the book, my reading flowed. As the story was precise and the style clear, I no longer hesitated in narrating, blow by blow, the torturous existence of that me. And regardless of how much that creature suffered, Kriska showed little commiseration. For although she had a certain affection for the me in the book, it was its inhumane creator with whom she was enchanted. And alone with her in the half-light of the smoky room, I actually convinced myself that I was the true author of the book. I took pleasure in the turns of phrase, the melody of my Hungarian, was enraptured by my voice. Fast, Kósta, faster, said Kriska, when I spent too long on the episodes in Rio de Janeiro. But when it was her turn to figure in the story, she asked me to reread the page, just once more, Kósta, again. And she laughed and laughed as if I were writing with a feather on her skin, this revolving disco, truly incredible. Somewhere towards the end, I knew she would change her position in bed in order to lean her head on my shoulder. She lay on her side in bed and leant her head on my shoulder, knowing that, without interrupting my reading, I enjoyed seeing the outline of her hips under her nightie. Then she subtly moved one leg over the other, making the shape of her thighs clear under the silk. And the next instant she became self-conscious, because now I was reading the book at the same time as the book was taking place. Dear Kriska, I asked, did you know that for you alone for nights on end I conceived the book that now draws to a close? I don't know what she was thinking, because she shut her eyes, but she nodded her head. And my beloved, of whose milk I had partaken, made me drink from the water in which she had washed her blouse.

A NOTE ON THE TYPE

The text of this book is set in Linotype Janson. The
original types were cut in about 1690 by Nicholas Kis,
a Hungarian working in Amsterdam. The face was
misnamed after Anton Janson, a Dutchman who worked
at the Ehrhardt Foundry in Leipzig, where the original
Kis types were kept in the early eighteenth century.
Monotype Ehrhardt is based on Janson. The original
matrices survived in Germany and were acquired in
1919 by the Stempel Foundry. Hermann Zapf used
these originals to redesign some of the weights
and sizes for Stempel. This Linotype version
was designed to follow the original types
under the direction of C. H. Griffith.